A LITTLE BOY'S BLUES
A Play in Three Acts

By Stacy Lamar King

Copyright © 2023 by Stacy Lamar King

A LITTLE BOY'S BLUES

All rights reserved.

No part of this publication may be reproduced or transmitted in any form or by any means electronic or mechanical, including photocopy, recording, or any information storage and retrieval system now known or invented, without permission in writing from the publisher, except by a reviewer who wishes to quote brief passages in connection with a review written for inclusion in a magazine, newspaper, or broadcast.

Print ISBN: 979-8-35091-835-9
eBook ISBN: 979-8-35091-836-6

Printed in the United States of America

CAST OF CHARACTERS

Little Boy: A mercurial 12-year-old with a mysterious case of the blues

Radio: A teenaged boy about 15 years old.

Hydraulic: A man in his 40's. Radio's father.

Lisa: A young girl about 11 years old from New Orleans.

Otis: A homeless veteran in his mid-30's

Brooklyn: A young lady about 17 years old.

Sister Girl: Little Boy's big little sister. A girl about 13 years old.

Little Brother: Little Boy's little brother. A boy about 9 years old.

Mika: A girl about 11 years old. A beautiful spirit.

Reverend: A man in his 60's.

Paul: A young boy about 12 years old.

Lyfe: A man of unknown age.

SCENE: THE QUEEN CITY
TIME: SUMMER 1979

ACT 1

Scene 1

Lisa

SETTING: HUMBOLDT PARK. A park had been a silent witness to the comings and goings of many a diverse people.

Today, she was a shell of her former glory. Her beauty covered by layers of neglect. The wrinkles and scars were visible for everyone to see.

Right in the middle of the park was an old, weathered bench made of iron and faded wood. Standing at ease and at its rear, was a solitary tree accompanied by an elderly streetlight, standing to its left, just a shade behind.

The two sentries had stood watch over the bench for decades, silent partners who had never spoken a word.

At RISE: LITTLE BOY sits alone on the bench holding his good friend WANDA gently in his hands. She was his old Earth, his crutch. A reminder that he was not alone. Wanda would never, ever, leave him.

She looked like a relic to some, junk to most, but she was everything to LITTLE BOY. A book with a worn cover. Something someone had given up on.

LITTLE BOY found her lying out with the trash. She was a treasure by any other name.

The moment he saw her he knew she had a million stories to tell, and he couldn't wait to replace her missing strings, so he could hear the first words.

WANDA was a little rough around the edges, but the two of them fit, they both had scars. Some visible, others not so visible.

WANDA was the only thing LITTLE BOY had ever called his own. On his good days, when his demons rested, he called her Cat, because plucking her strings made him think of the girl he still saw in his dreams. The one who still haunted him.

A girl with the most amazing green and auburn eyes. A girl who appeared almost every night and disappeared before he woke. She was there and then she was gone and his thoughts of her were bittersweet.

Lost in those thoughts. He sat and worked on a new song. Why? He didn't know. He played the notes as they appeared in his mind.

(She walked right out of the Bayou.)

LISA

Whatcha playing boy?

LITTLE BOY

(Without missing a beat or even looking up.) The Blues.

LISA

The Blues!?!? (LISA's voice was a mixture of both excitement and curiosity.)

LITTLE BOY

Yeah, the Blues.

LISA

Boy, what do you know about the blues?

LITTLE BOY

I know a lot. (As a matter of fact.) My Grandpa says the blues are the feelings you get when you can't explain a story that won't stop playing in your mind.

LISA

Huhhhh? What are you talking about?

LISA chuckled, her spirit causing LITTLE BOY to crack the signature half smile that would later become his trademark. The very smile that only those close to him could see. It was the last glimmer of hope, that in spite of it all, still remained with him.

LITTLE BOY

Best I can explain it. At times its both scary and exciting.

LISA

Truth be told, that sounds a lot like confusion, if you ask me. Well, that's what my Nana would've told your grandpa if he had told her that old wives' tale, because she's the truth.

LITTLE BOY stopped strumming the guitar long enough to look up at her. He didn't realize it while she was talking, but when he saw her, he knew deep down inside that the million or so actions that his grandpa told him were required to bring two souls together had just completed a cycle. His grandpa was always right. This was how souls met.

LISA

Are you OK? Why you are sitting there with your mouth wide open like that? You trying to catch that fly? Don't tell me. Let me guess. It's the blues... (LISA laughed her laugh.)

LISA's laugh was so pure. So innocent and infectious. LITTLE BOY had no choice but to laugh along with her when he heard it. Right then he knew, when he heard her laugh, that she was feeling OK This was an event in and of itself because LITTLE BOY rarely laughed at all.

LITTLE BOY

I don't know what just happened. I was looking at your face and I heard you talking. Then out of the blue my grandpa popped in my mind. All I heard after that were the crickets.

LISA waltzed over and plopped down, right next to LITTLE BOY. She wasn't aware of his rules about his personal space. There was an area around him that LITTLE BOY just didn't let anyone penetrate. When people did, their actions, even when innocent, hurt more than they helped.

LISA was so close that LITTLE BOY felt like he was wearing her shadow like a sweater. It was a little irritating but LITTLE BOY knew he wouldn't win this battle, so he took the high road and embraced the moment. At least that's the way the story would be told to their children.

LITTLE BOY
I take it you've never been "confused" before? (LITTLE BOY used air quotations to accentuate LISA's word, confused.) I guess you've never felt like your world was upside down? (This was the world that LITTLE BOY lived in.)

LISA
Hmmm… I don't know. Maybe. I guess so.

LITTLE BOY
Whew. I hope all your answers aren't going to be like that.

LISA
Oh, boy hush. Deal with it.

LITTLE BOY
(LITTLE BOY shook his head. Intrinsically knowing her words to be right and exact. A precursor for how their relationship would

always be.) Well, I live with the blues. In fact, I don't remember the time before them. It seems to me, the blues are all I've ever known.

LISA

Oh, you got lost in the sauce. That's something we're going to have to work on. (She didn't know this would be a lifetime commitment.) Life ain't supposed to be like that. Anyway, what's the name of that song you were just playing?

LITTLE BOY

I call it Wanda.

LISA

Oh, a girl. (A shade of disappointment.) Sounds like you like her. (Temporarily deflated.)

LITTLE BOY

I think so.

LISA

YOU THINK SO!!! (LISA was surprised.)

LITTLE BOY

Yeah, I think so. Why'd you say it like that?

LISA

Because when you play her song, she's written all over your face. (She reached over and wrote WANDA across his forehead.) Listen up boy, a girl wants a boy that knows what he likes, not one whose all wishy washy, sounding like he could take her or leave her. I can see why you're always playing the blues, it sounds like you met the girl of your dreams and had no idea what to say to her.

LITTLE BOY

First off, I never said I met her, and I most certainly didn't tell you that I dreamed about her. All I said was her name. Truth be told, I saw her one time from a distance, at the train station, and before I could find the courage to walk over and say hello, her train pulled up, and like that she was gone. I hesitated. I froze. I guess I didn't believe I deserved anything that beautiful in my life.

LISA

Awweeee mannnnn, that sounds so sad. She could have been the one. You know, your everything.

LITTLE BOY

MY EVERYTHING??? (LITTLE BOY spoke the words like this was the first time he had ever considered them.)

LISA

Yes, your everything, the one you can't wait to see every day after school. The one you share your candy with. The one that makes you feel like you're the most important person in any world. Real or imagined.

LITTLE BOY

Is that what your everything feels like to you?

LISA

When I meet him. I'll let you know.

LITTLE BOY

Oh. You haven't met. You know what? I'm not going to let that happen to me again. I won't freeze the next time. She could have been my everything, just like you said. Now she's gone and I'll never know. (LITTLE BOY looked off into the distance. For a moment he allowed himself to believe that his blues started with her.)

LISA

Yeah, don't freeze next time. (LISA wondered why she told LITTLE BOY that she could have been his everything.) Girls like boys who know what they want even when they don't? Your face is still blue though. It's not just her, is it?

LITTLE BOY

Nope. There's more. I really don't like talking about it.

LISA

We gotta change that too. How am I going to fix you if you don't talk to me? You gotta talk to somebody and since I'm here, why not me? (LISA shrugged.)

LITTLE BOY

Tell you what. How about I let my music do the talking today. Listen closely, I think this will help answer some of your questions.

(LITTLE BOY played a few chords from a different song. This was his song, A Little Boy's Blues.)

LISA

That's cool. You talk with your hands. That's a start. It's a little different though. But I can dig it. Sounds like a dreamy mystery. What's it about?

LITTLE BOY

Wow, how did you know that? It is a dream. I have it all the time. It's a dream about a man I've never met. A man I've been looking for all my life. Funny thing he's even hard to find in my dreams. (Shaking his head.) I never see his face and he never speaks. (LITTLE BOY shook his head out of frustration.) But you know what, I was born with my imagination and these hands and this guitar found me. I figure it all has to mean something, right?

LISA

Everything means something Little Boy.

LITTLE BOY

Dreaming at night was always a nightmare but during the day I was awake in those dreams, I could see the shadow of his face and when he spoke, I heard his voice for the first time. It was amazing. Close your eyes and listen to what he sounds like.

(LISA closed her eyes and LITTLE BOY stood in front of her and played a few more chords from the song he called Heaven.)

LISA

Ooh, that's nice. You're good. I mean like all grown-up kinda good. Play me some more. Pleaseeeeee.

                          LITTLE BOY
OK. But you gotta promise me that you won't laugh.

                             LISA
Promises.

(LISA flashed her million-watt smile for the second time that day. LITTLE BOY's heart paused for a moment as he took it all in.)

                          LITTLE BOY
This here is what he looks like.

LITTLE BOY played a different rift. As he played, LITTLE BOY could feel the brightness of LISA's smile through his eyelids. He always closed his eyes when he played from the heart. LISA imagined it had to be a Queen City thing because no one closed their eyes around strangers in Nawlins.

                             LISA
He sounds handsome.

                          LITTLE BOY
You can see him, right?

                             LISA
(LISA nodded.) Yessssss.

                          LITTLE BOY
What does he look like?

LISA

He has a big ole Kool-Aid smile. A lot different than that crooked one you're wearing right now. He doesn't hold back like you do. He reminds me of you. I want to hear it all.

LITTLE BOY

Ok, I haven't finished it, this is all that's left. I've never shared this part with anyone. Not even my grandpa.

LISA was just beginning to understand just how much LITTLE BOY trusted her and how much trust meant to him. LITTLE BOY sat next to her and began to play the rest of A Little Boy's Blues. LISA knew he was sitting there but he was no longer with her. A part of him had gone somewhere else.

Perhaps to the place the broken go to when they try to heal themselves. His flow was both happy and sad and hearing it brought smiles and tears to their little brown faces. She was beginning to understand his ways. How he dealt with the world. She felt his sadness for the first time. It was so heavy.

LISA

That ain't THE BLUES Little Boy. I don't know what that is. That's too heavy for the blues. That's something else.

LITTLE BOY

It's what I play. I don't know what to call it either. People call it all kind of things. Mostly the blues. That's what I was trying to tell you earlier.

LISA

I get it now. It's blueish but it ain't blue. Some of it is pretty black. Is the man your father?

LITTLE BOY

Huh? What? Oh, the man in my dreams. Yeah, how did you know that?

LITTLE BOY's voice was suddenly weak and trembling. LISA could see the cracks in the mask he wore around others. She could see through his veil. She saw the LITTLE BOY that wasn't quite sure if he belonged in this world. More than anything else, she could sense his pain, it was as if he were caught between two worlds. Barely present in one and curious about, but not quite sure of how to get to the other.

LISA

Girls know fathers. What did he say to you?

LITTLE BOY

He says the same things every time. He tells me he loves and misses me. Then he kneels to look at me, his eyes searching mine for something. He looks until he finds a part of him in my eyes. Every time he finds it, he pauses and lets out the loudest laugh I've ever heard. Then he shouts "yeah there's my boy." It's never a regular laugh. No ma'am, it's one of those big ole belly laughs. (LITTLE BOY tried to laugh like his father, but he sounded like an old man who was running out of air.)

LISA laughed at LITTLE BOY's laugh. The mask was off briefly And she saw him. But just as quickly as LITTLE BOY started laughing, he stopped, and the mood became very serious. He put the mask back on. She held his hands and looked directly into his eyes. He was shaking. (She knew this little boy was going to be complicated. Their story would be an unbalanced mixture of sun and rain, mostly rain.)

LITTLE BOY

(Composing himself. Sniffling.) Then, he tells me that he's so sorry. In the beginning, I didn't understand why. He says he's sorry because he knows he will never be a part of any of the real memories that I make in this life. And just like that he always stops talking and turns and begins to walk away. It's so quiet, I can hear his tears hitting the ground and they sound like waves crashing against the rocks. I don't know how long he's been crying like this. I imagine forever. All I do know is that every time it rains really hard, I can't help but think about his tears. His steps become lighter and lighter the farther he walks away from me. The tears get more faint with each step. And right before it goes totally silent, he pauses and turns around and says to me, "Little Boy you can always find me here in your daydreams and when you play your song. I'll be listening for it."

The LITTLE BOY who had become a Little Man long before his time, began to cry. LISA knew this moment was different because he couldn't stop. She hugged and consoled him. Neither saying a word. She had no idea that he had never cried before. He couldn't and he didn't know why.

LISA

You got to get it out baby boy. It's OK to cry. You can always let it out around me. For real. I promise I will always be here for you.

You feel everything all the time. I know you're going to help a lot of people. But you're going to need someone to help you too.

LITTLE BOY

You don't think I'm weird?

LISA

Now I didn't say that. I'm kidding. No. I get you. You're unique. Most won't get you because they can't, but don't worry about them. The ones that need you will get you.

LITTLE BOY

Thank you. Your words made me feel better. I like your words. I don't know your name. What is it?

LISA

It's Lisa.

LITTLE BOY

Lisaaaaaa. You don't sound like people from around here. Nah, you got a different sound. Like a new guitar with old strings. My Grandpa would probably say "Little Boy that girl right there. she got an old soul." Where you from?

LISA

Nawlins.

LITTLE BOY

Huh? Say that one more time.

LISA

New. Orleans.

(LISA pronounced every syllable as if she were talking to a baby.)

LITTLE BOY

OK, I got it, I'm not a baby though. If it's called New Orleans, why did you call it Nawlins?

LISA

That's just how we talk man. Anyway, if you were a real Blues Man, you would have known the answer to your question.

LITTLE BOY

Well, I guess I'm not a real "Blues Man." So, why don't you explain it to me Miss Nawlins.

LISA

Nawlins, Little Boy, is the home of the Blues. Come on man every Blues Man is supposed to know that.

LITTLE BOY

Oh, I knew that. (In his best Nawlins twang.)

(They sat and laughed like twins. His laugh was so pure. But different than LISA's. When LITTLE BOY laughed, he was usually masking something else.)

LITTLE BOY

I feel like you have come all the way from Nawlins to tell me something.

LISA

Well, ain't you just full of yourself Mister. I barely know you Little Boy.

LITTLE BOY

Listen closely. I'm going to tell you a diddy. Pay attention. Here I go. Most people spend their entire lifetime doing one of these two things. Hating the present or reliving the past, over, and over again.

LISA

OK, who told you that and why are you telling me?

LITTLE BOY

Does it matter who told me? Promise me you won't do either.

(LITTLE BOY took LISA by the shoulders and looked straight into her eyes.)

LITTLE BOY

Promise Me. (He was serious.)

LISA

OK, I promise. Can you tell me what it means?

LITTLE BOY

It means if you live your life scared to make a mistake or you spend all your time thinking about mistakes you've already made, you won't go anywhere. You'll stay stuck. You'll be miserable. So, once again Miss Nawlins, what did you come all the way from Nawlins to tell little ole me?

LISA

Oh no, a guitar player and a psychic. We got a lot of them in Nawlins. Show me something. Why don't you tell me what I came here to tell you.

LITTLE BOY

Because it doesn't work like that. You walked right out of Bayou to get something off your chest. (LISA looked surprised.) Oh, you didn't know I knew about the Bayou. (He chuckled.) You told me we have to let go of the past. Isn't that what you said? You told me you would make a safe place for me to do that. I can do the same for you. But you have to talk to me. I'm all ears now.

(LITTLE BOY placed his hands over his tiny ears.)

LISA

More like all head if you ask me.

LITTLE BOY

Huh? Whatcha say?

LISA

Oh nothing. (LISA flashed a crooked smile just like LITTLE BOY's. It felt strange on her face.) Alright, I came up here to tell you I'm stuck, and I'm scared and I'm tired of feeling both.

LITTLE BOY

That's hard to believe. You're so strong. What could scare you?

LISA

My father.

LITTLE BOY

Why?

LISA

Like you I never met him, and I keep thinking all the time. What if he has another daughter and she's like your Wanda? She's his EVERYTHING. I can't go there like you. Dream about it and all. Your story will always be a mystery. Not mine. My father has always been close enough to hug me, but he won't. And I don't understand why. It's gone on so long that I don't want to know why anymore. So, I cover up my pain with things that hurt me more than this big hole he left in my heart. So, what's worst Little Boy? Being unlovable or being unable to love?

LITTLE BOY

Do I have to choose? They both hurt.

LISA

I know that. Which one hurts the most?

LITTLE BOY

I don't know, but if I met them both, the one who wasn't loved and the one who couldn't love, I would feel and respect the pain of each. I hope that makes sense.

LISA

Yeah. Kinda.

LITTLE BOY

You feel like you're stuck between them, don't you?

LISA

Yeah, I do.

LITTLE BOY

I know that feeling. OK what else am I missing?

LISA

Who said you were missing anything?

LITTLE BOY

I'm saying it. If we're going to be friends, let's be friends. There's something else you want to tell me. I can feel it.

LISA

Hmmmm. You and your feelings Little Boy. What if I told you how hard it is to be good, do good, or even see any good in anything, when you don't feel good. Or what if I told you that feeling bad feels better than feeling nothing at all. Would you try to understand me or would you just stand back and talk about me to others? (LISA moved on before LITTLE BOY could answer.)

LISA

People call Nawlins sin city. It's a place full of bad boys and girls like me. So how could I ever meet a good boy when the only boys I know, are bad like me? And if I did meet a good one what could I offer him? All I know how to be is bad.

LITTLE BOY

First, I need you to breathe and relax. Then I want you to listen to what you came to hear from me. You're not bad Lisa. Just a little broken. You deserve to be loved and you can love.

(LITTLE BOY picked up his guitar and began to play.)

LISA

Who were you talking to?

LITTLE BOY

The father of all the lost children.

LISA

What did he say?

LITTLE BOY

He said He didn't make a mistake when He made you. He said He placed something beautiful inside you. A heart so big that it will allow you to love others unconditionally. You're going to make mistakes and some people are going to hurt you. But don't change. He made a boy for you. You won't meet him until he's a man. A man who is going to tear down the walls you've built around your heart. He told me to tell you there are little girls all around this world who are waiting to hear you sing your song through your words. When you share your story especially the hard parts, many broken hearts will begin to heal because you spoke love to them. He called your song "My Lovely Little Lisa." Do you want to hear the rest?

LISA

Yessssssssssss.

LITTLE BOY stood up on the bench, put on his shades, and began to pluck the strings of his guitar. LISA had never seen this side of LITTLE BOY. This was the entertainer in him. He plucked and plucked until he heard the notes that were being sent to him from on high. What came next, was the part of the song, that only LISA could understand.

When LITTLE BOY finished, he sat on the bench. He was exhausted. LISA noticed and closed the gap between them. She hugged him, he hugged her right back, and they sat and faced one another. Their foreheads touched and they held hands, healing each other for that moment. They knew then that they would be forever friends.

(BLACKOUT)

(END OF SCENE)

ACT 1

Scene 2
Otis

SETTING:

What is innocence? When is it lost? And if it is lost, can it ever be found again?

There are a million Otis' in this world. Young men who have stood up under the guise of patriotism and been chewed up and spit out as shells of their former selves.

Men, who on the surface appear to have paid an extraordinary price for nothing more than their entrance into this thing called life at the wrong time. A price they have paid with their bodies, hearts, and minds.

It was a Saturday morning in late Spring, somewhere between Memorial Day and the end of the school year. This was the perennial sentence that was uniquely LITTLE BOY's.

Three months in the yard was the reprieve the warden of The Academy granted LITTLE BOY each year. It marked the end of another season of lies where he was forced to listen to tales about his story.

The actual time on the clock was somewhere between the third School House Rock song and the end of Saturday morning's cartoons.

This was LITTLE BOY's favorite time of year. This was his place of innocence.

At RISE: LITTLE BOY is seated on his favorite bench. Accompanied by Wanda and a small brown paper bag stuffed with his favorite penny candies.

He sits daydreaming, with his eyes closed, still ignoring the warning of LISA, choosing instead to feel the warmth of the sun on the eyelids of his little brown face, thinking about the one who made them both.

OTIS enters the park from stage left. He has a walk that defies gravity. LITTLE BOY described it just as his Uncle Benny would have if he saw OTIS.

OTIS had what Uncle Benny would call, a little hitch in his get along. To LITTLE BOY, OTIS walked as if his legs had been bolted on the wrong side.

The other kids laughed at OTIS when they saw him walk, calling his swagger the drunken style. A style made famous in many of the dollar show karate flicks they often frequented on Saturday afternoons.

From time to time, LITTLE BOY also heard the old heads utter terms that were not quite so endearing. They whispered nothing sweet about OTIS when he passed on by.

Their comments always bothered LITTLE BOY. They were mean and unnecessary. Every time he heard them, he got angry. He couldn't help it. He felt every injustice of those who couldn't or wouldn't fight for themselves.

If you watched OTIS long enough, every third or fourth step looked like it would be his last, as if he would fall flat on his face. Only to be amazed that he still stood upright, as if held by an invisible hand.

And so, it was, that after this series of animated "steps and missteps" that OTIS found himself standing or swaying, depending on your point of reference, directly in front of the Little Boy with the Blues.

Coincidence?

OTIS
Soul Train you out here awfully early this morning. You got something on your mind?

LITTLE BOY
No Sir Mister Otis. Just daydreaming.

OTIS

About what?

LITTLE BOY

I was wondering why more don't kids don't like to read. I just don't get it. I love reading. But they laugh at me when they see me with my books. Don't they know that a book can take you anywhere in the world for free? It's like they're scared to leave here. Where is the imagination in this world?

OTIS

Ohhhhhh, you one of them big thinkers. I see. You got a point there. But listen up before you become a judge. You're the only one that can see through your eyes. They can't see what you see, and you can't see what they see. You might want to cut them some slack.

LITTLE BOY

I never thought of it like that.

OTIS

Listen, young blood, a lot of kids have been dealt some bad hands out here. If you know what I mean.

LITTLE BOY

I'm sorry but I don't.

OTIS

Listen close. Life is like a poker hand. Some kids get dealt a royal flush. They get their mom, their dad, the white picket fence, a dog, and enough love to be happy. Other kids get dealt the hand no one wants, some before they can even walk, and they struggle every day just to put a smile on their face in the morning. Do you understand what I'm saying about the cards you're dealt?

LITTLE BOY

I think so.

OTIS

Maybe what you see from them is the best they can show you. Learn to listen to their songs, their words, without judging them. Then you will hear their truth and that's what matters.

LITTLE BOY

I never looked at it that way.

OTIS

It's OK, these things you'll learn over time because you're a big thinker. Now I heard that you can really play that there guitar. Young fella, bass player named Jimmy McKnight. Tall, slim, dark-skinned fella. Got the brightest teeth I ever saw. Hangs out Saturday evenings at the Blue Note. But that's neither here nor there.

LITTLE BOY

Huh?

OTIS

Figure of speech. He drives this longgggg money green deuce and a quarter. Do you know who I'm talking about?

LITTLE BOY

I don't know him, but I've seen that car. It is so cool.

OTIS

Yeah, that's a bad car. He ain't the most dependable of sorts with his stories if you know what I mean. His memory doesn't work that well after noon. But that's alright. My old man used to say even a broken clock is right twice a day.

LITTLE BOY

That's funny.

OTIS

So, let's see if there's any truth to what he said about your magic fingers. Let me hear you play something. I got a good ear for the blues.

LITTLE BOY

I just play whatever pops into my mind. Some people say it sounds like the blues. I'm twelve and I can't say if it does or doesn't. The notes kinda write themselves in my mind and my little fingers, why, they're just along for the ride. Trying to keep up. You dig?

(Otis laughed at LITTLE BOY's first attempt at being cool.)

LITTLE BOY couldn't help but intently at OTIS. He could only imagine the stories that were hidden behind the eyes that were looking at him.

At times he caught himself staring and when he did, he quickly looked away. Otis' face glowed like soft gold. He looked much younger than LITTLE BOY had imagined. It was hard to tell from afar and no one ever got that close to him. This was the first time LITTLE BOY had ever spoken to OTIS.

OTIS

You don't talk like a little boy. Sounds like you have seen some things in this life.

LITTLE BOY

Not a lot, but there are some things I wish I could forget. We all get dealt a hand we didn't ask for. I talk to God.

OTIS

Ah you on the right path. Now I see you. (OTIS looked at LITTLE BOY and nodded his head in affirmation.) I been on the path too. Might not look like it. Hanging on by a thread. Most would say by the skin of my teeth.

LITTLE BOY

But you're still hanging.

OTIS

Yeahhhhhhh. Still hanging on. You know, when I was young, a little older than you are right now, I really thought I was going to be somebody.

LITTLE BOY

You are somebody.

OTIS

Never in a million years did I imagine I would end up like this. No Sir, not me. I had me some big ole dreams Little Boy. I was gonna grab this world by its tail and just shake it up. (OTIS shook an imaginary lion.) Yes indeed. I wasn't going to let nothing hold me back. You know why?

(LITTLE BOY shrugged his small shoulders.)

OTIS

Because I was somebody back then. I was Kenny the King of the beats. You wouldn't even recognize me then. I was a bad man. But somebody up there had different plans for me. (OTIS shook his head and laughed one of those old man laughs. It must have been an inside joke.)

LITTLE BOY

You mean your name isn't Otis?

OTIS

Oh no, that ain't my name. That's just what they call me out here in these streets because of my situation. I'll never be Kenny again. He's buried Little Boy. I keep him locked away. Deep down inside my heart where no one can hurt him again. Because there ain't no place in this world for something that beautiful.

LITTLE BOY

Beautiful like Thelma from Good Times?

OTIS

(Otis laughed.) Nooooo not like that. More like the beauty of a single red rose standing all by itself in a big ole lot full of trash.

LITTLE BOY

Wow.

OTIS

Kinda, puts your mind in a headlock, doesn't it? At first, you wonder, there? But why is it there? When you really think about it, you begin to wonder about who put it there. It can make you dizzy thinking about it.

(OTIS shook his head and shot his eyes up towards the Heavens.)

LITTLE BOY

My mind is spinning just thinking about that.

OTIS

Yeah, that would be the headlock. You look at that rose and at first you think it doesn't stand a chance. How could it?

LITTLE BOY

I know. It seems impossible.

OTIS

Bingo. I didn't get it until He covered my rose with all my trash. He makes the impossible possible.

LITTLE BOY

Is that a riddle?

OTIS

It's my story.

LITTLE BOY

You got layers Mister Otis.

OTIS

Yeah. Layers.

LITTLE BOY

When I was a little boy. An old blind lady asked me if she could hold my hand. (OTIS chuckled at LITTLE BOY'S reference to his youth.) I said yes and she did. She said, "Little Boy you will never know which pair of eyes the Good Lord will use to look at you." I didn't know what it meant, and she didn't explain. She was one of those kind. She knew she had changed me with the words. Those words made me treat every set of eyes looking at me like they were God's. She taught me the power of words Mr. Otis.

OTIS

That's a powerful story.

LITTLE BOY

Do you mind if I call you Mister Kenny instead of Mister Otis?

OTIS

I don't see why not. But only when no one's around. Everybody doesn't need to know my story. You dig?

LITTLE BOY

I dig. Thanks for sharing your story with me. A rose is still a rose, even when it's surrounded by trash. That story has good bones.

OTIS

Oh, you see through the right eye.

LITTLE BOY

I suppose so. I come from a family of storytellers. It made me a lil different. Always thinking about things. Some things kids shouldn't have to think about. Like the lies grown-ups tell and the secrets they keep.

OTIS

That's never cool.

LITTLE BOY

I had to cover up my rose too. And I learned how to act and talk so people would leave me alone.

OTIS

You understand. You got a big heart. I can tell. I bet you feel everything.

LITTLE BOY

Yeah, I do. I don't have the words to explain it. If I don't feel what other people are feeling I don't feel much of anything. It takes me to a place that's hard to leave because I'm so used to being there alone by myself.

OTIS

My old man, bless his soul, used to say this world just wants its ears tickled. Every time he said that I laughed because at the time it sounded so funny.

LITTLE BOY

It does sound funny. My ears feel itchy now.

OTIS

Then he explained what it meant. He said people only want to hear what makes them feel good and nothing else. Then I stopped laughing. Take it from me Little Boy. The longer you spend acting like someone else the harder it becomes to be yourself. You can also get lost when you're all alone, and let me tell you, once you get lost, there aren't enough doctors or pills to put you back together so you can find yourself.

OTIS could feel himself getting angry and for a moment he was back in that hospital. They both looked at his balled-up fists. LITTLE BOY tapped his hand and OTIS snapped out of it. He had transported again.

OTIS

You got His light in you, and it shines so bright, that it's going to cast shadows on others. Reminding them of things they pretend they never did. They're going to look at you but never understand you because they don't understand the light that's in you. I do. But you gotta stop looking for people to love you if they don't love the light inside you. You got me?

LITTLE BOY

Yes Sir. (With a salute and a smile.) Mister Kenny, are you still going to shake up the world?

OTIS

Every day Tiny Trooper.

(LITTLE BOY laughed.)

LITTLE BOY

How so?

OTIS

By the grace of God. He wakes me up and gives me another set of orders even if I screwed up the ones, He gave me the day before. He doesn't keep score and He never gives up on me.

LITTLE BOY

That's amazing Mister Kenny.

OTIS

Each day is a mystery because I never know who I'm going to meet or what I'm supposed to say. But I walk wherever He guides me and say whatever he tells me.

LITTLE BOY

Is that ever scary?

OTIS

Never. Not even when it should be. Sometimes they see me coming, most times they smell me before they see me, other times they hear me shucking and jiving and talking to myself, and because of the way He dressed me, they never touch me. It's their vanity. Funny thing about our senses, when we don't use them, we sort of forget how to. It's the most interesting thing.

LITTLE BOY

Like hugging. I hate it...

OTIS

You mean touching. I'm sure you have a reason for that. I used to think that my memories of touch would make the fear people have of touching me too much for me to bear. But the longer I walked this path I began to understand how their fear of touching me kept a lot of bad things from happening to me. The Good Lord works in mysterious ways. Don't worry too much about that hugging thing. It will work itself out. You'll understand it all one day.

LITTLE BOY

Sounds like a force field.

OTIS

Force field? What are you talking about Mister Scientific?

LITTLE BOY

That thing you're talking about. That protection of yours. How can I explain it? Ummmmm let's say you just happened to be sitting in the cafeteria at a table all by yourself, not because no one likes you or anything like that, out of respect, because they know you like your space. But right across from your fortress there's a table of spitballers who think you're different, a nerd, a weirdo of sorts. They're preparing to do what spitballers do, and there's just you and them and you both know what's about to happen next. But this time you have this invisible, impenetrable barrier all around you and their spitballs can't get to you. That Mister Kenny is a forcefield.

OTIS

Interesting. A detailed explanation for sure. Thanks for the explanation. So, tell me how did that forcefield work out for you?

LITTLE BOY

Huh, me? You thought I was talking about me getting hit with spitballs? Oh no that's not a true story. That was a metaphor.

OTIS

Oh. You made me feel like I was right there in your fortress. Spitballs flying and everything.

OTIS looked down at his feet and laughed like he hadn't laughed in years. LITTLE BOY tried to hold back but there was no stopping this laughing wave. He had never told anyone this part of his story before. The bullying you must endure when you're different.

OTIS

You feel that?

LITTLE BOY

What? Spitballs?

OTIS

Nooooo, much better than that.

LITTLE BOY

A forcefield?

OTIS

No, the weight that was just lifted off your shoulders young man. You really needed to talk about that with someone. You're not alone. Kids have always done cruel things.

(LITTLE BOY giggled nervously. He still had years left on his school sentence.)

LITTLE BOY

Yeah, I did. Mister Kenny, where are you going when you leave here?

OTIS

Wherever these feet take me. The good Lord picks em up and sets em down and all I do is lean back and strut. You know what I mean?

LITTLE BOY

Oh, that's what it's called. You mean you walk like that on purpose? (OTIS laughed again. Only this time it was one of those big bellied laughs like LITTLE BOY's Grandpa.)

OTIS

Boy you gone make me bust a gut out here today. I ain't laughed like that in years. "You mean you walk like that on purpose?" I ain't never been asked that. You sure keep em coming. Those zingers of yours. I'm scared to ask you the next question.

LITTLE BOY

What's that?

OTIS

Did you think it was alcohol?

LITTLE BOY

That's what some people say. Personally, I thought God put your legs on the wrong side, just to see if we were paying attention.

OTIS

Whew another one. You something else Little Boy. (OTIS continued laughing.)

LITTLE BOY

Something else?

OTIS

You see the world through a very special pair of glasses.

LITTLE BOY

Glasses??? I don't wear glasses.

OTIS

It's a figure of speech. Means you see the world differently than most. Now bout my legs. I assure you they ain't on backwards. Look at my feet. Left foot, right foot. Been walking like this since the war. (LITTLE BOY looked on in amazement.) What I got in these legs is a whole lot of metal. They call it shrapnel. It was a parting gift from a party I should have never gone to.

LITTLE BOY

Where was the party at?

OTIS

Vietnam.

LITTLE BOY

Was it a surprise party?

OTIS

Yeah, you could say that. It was a big ole surprise to me. The worst party I have ever been invited to.

LITTLE BOY

Maybe you'll tell that story one day. The story about the surprise party that wasn't much of a party.

OTIS

Yeah, maybe one day. (OTIS looked off distantly lost for a moment in Vietnam. They called it the thousand-yard stare. LITTLE BOY didn't know what to say so he waited quietly and patiently for OTIS to return.)

OTIS

Now this shrapnel makes my legs do what they do. Sometimes they work right, most times they don't. But what am I gonna do? Cry over spilt milk? Not me, not Kenny the King. No Sir. My Pops didn't raise me like that. He said, "Son you gotta play the hand ya dealt." You gotta get on with the get on. So, I keeps it moving the best I can. Now you know all my secrets. Can you keep this one too?

LITTLE BOY

Sir yes Sir!

OTIS

Oh my, a sir sandwich. I ain't heard one of those since I left the island.

LITTLE BOY waited for an explanation that didn't come. It appeared that Otis was one of the kind too.

OTIS

You gonna play me that song or what?

LITTLE BOY

Yes Sir. Anything for you Mister Kenny. Let me know what you think of the beginning?

OTIS

Sure, lay it on me.

(LITTLE BOY's fingers moved like they were on fire. It was electric.)

OTIS

Now that's cool. I like that. It's like you flipped the blues inside out. It's gonna be really hard to call that there the blues. That's something else.

LITTLE BOY

What should I call it then?

OTIS

You can call that The Truth! No doubt about it. That's what it is. And the truth is going to set you free. That's your ticket out of here.

LITTLE BOY

You really think so?

OTIS

Yes, you know who gave you that sound.

LITTLE BOY

God?

OTIS

Most definitely. It's a wrap. You're guilty as charged.

LITTLE BOY

Guilty of what?

OTIS

Being loved by the Lord. And ain't nothing wrong with that. That's what you want. So how do you plead?

LITTLE BOY

Guilty Sir.

OTIS

Of what my man?

LITTLE BOY

BEING LOVED BY THE LORD!

OTIS

This is what you were created to do. Flip the blues inside out so you can help others through their storm. But before you can do that you have to be brave enough to let your rose stand tall in the trash. Don't hide yours like I did mine. This is who you are. You are the rose. Now hit me with that beat Soul Train.

LITTLE BOY played a little and OTIS danced a little. Then he played a little more and OTIS danced a little more. They continued this duet until OTIS' song was done. When they finished OTIS also had a brand-new dance. He walked a little different.

The two laughed together more than they had ever laughed apart. OTIS' mission from the Lord for this day had been accomplished. He had gone where his feet were directed and spoke to the one the Lord placed in front of him.

After the last note the warrior and the little boy with the blues stood and saluted one another. Then OTIS did an about face, leaned back, and strutted, like he was back on the D.I Avenue on that island for the very first time, young and innocent, living the dream he had before the surprise party over in Vietnam.

(BLACKOUT)

(END OF SCENE)

ACT 1

Scene 3
Radio

SETTING: LITTLE BOY arrived at the bus stop extra early this morning. It was Friday and he knew his neighborhood hero would appear at any moment now, gliding to the bus stop on the other side of the tracks. This was the highlight of LITTLE BOY's day.

Like clockwork, as LITTLE BOY looked far off in the distance, he saw RADIO, strolling down the boulevard, wrapped in his razor-sharp Levi's, black on white striped shell-toed Adidas, a silver "Radio" buckle, a fresh Bob Marley T-Shirt, and an afro so fresh and so clean-clean, that both the afro and the barber were known by that very name.

If this were a movie, this would be the part where they filmed the superhero moving in super slow motion, floating down the avenue as if on air, boom box in hand, blasting his theme song, waking up everyone in the neighborhood, and receiving nothing but love.

This wasn't that kind of movie. The block were sleepy and LITTLE BOY and RADIO were the only two on it. Everyone called him RADIO. He was the smoothest brother in town. No one knew his real name. Even the old people called him RADIO.

His voice was magic. It was part parts Louie Armstrong, Floyd Geiger, Barry White, and Don Cornelius.

LITTLE BOY didn't know how he got the voice, but he knew when he reached RADIO's age, he wanted one just like it.

RADIO cruised right into the bus stop, geared down, dropped his levitation, and LITTLE BOY marveled as his feet actually touched the ground.

Everything about RADIO was fly. He moved like there was a camera following him. For a split second, it even appeared like he looked across the street and nodded towards LITTLE BOY.

LITTLE BOY thought to himself "No way, this couldn't be." So, he turned around to make sure no one had snuck up behind him.

The RADIO's of this world, the ones from the other side of the tracks, with the fresh clothes and new kicks never stopped to talk to the misfits in retreads who hailed from LITTLE BOY's side.

But this wasn't a movie. This was life and life had no script.

At RISE: Appearing extremely confident of his place in this world, RADIO reached down on the boom box he called Techtonik and pressed play. The lyrics to Sister Sledge's "He's the Greatest Dancer" jumped out the speakers, ran across the street, and introduced themselves into LITTLE BOY's soul.

They were words to most, but words were everything to LITTLE BOY. It was an unexpected introduction, and LITTLE BOY had to acknowledge within his spirit that he finally had words and a dance for his beloved WANDA. That is if their paths should ever cross again. If a little boy could dance, he could hope.

After watching a huge smile envelop LITTLE BOY'S face, RADIO pressed stop and motioned with his hand for LITTLE BOY to come across the tracks.

LITTLE BOY, realizing that RADIO was really talking to him this time, ran across. When he reached him, RADIO ejected the tape, and placed it in a specially marked cassette case he had labeled "The Little Blue's Man."

RADIO

This one's for you Little Man. (RADIO handed the case to LITTLE BOY.) You're a cool little dude and I dig your style. It's so different. Unique is the word I'm reaching for. I like your style a lot, brother.

LITTLE BOY looked at RADIO with astonishment and awe. He was speechless. RADIO knew he existed. The words were the most LITTLE BOY had ever heard RADIO speak, and he had spoken them all to him.

LITTLE BOY

Thank you, Radio. (With much reverence.) I love your voice, Radio. It's the coolest. It's so dope.

RADIO

Oh, you got jokes Little Man.

LITTLE BOY

Nooooooo. I'm for real. When I'm your age I want my voice to be just like yours.

RADIO

Nahhh, you don't want that Little Man. Trust me when I tell you that. But thanks for being kind about it. Funny thing, I didn't know you could speak. Word on the streets, is that you only spoke with your hands.

LITTLE BOY

That's funny Radio, I thought you only spoke to people like yourself, you know. Only to the other cool boys, with special powers like yours.

RADIO

We might have never spoken if we had both kept thinking like that.

BOTH BOYS

THAT'S CRAZY! I KNOW! We just said the same thing. We did it again. I KNOW! STOP. You first. No, you first. (As they stood pointing towards one another.)

(They even laughed at the same time. Kindred spirits. Like brothers. The universe speaks if you listen closely.)

RADIO

Yo Little Man I needed that laugh.

LITTLE BOY

Me too Radio.

RADIO

I haven't laughed like that since the accident.

LITTLE BOY

I haven't laughed like that ever. (They laughed together again.) You had an accident?

RADIO

Yeah, that's how I got this "magic" voice you like so much.

LITTLE BOY

You had a regular voice, like mine Radio?

RADIO

Yeah man, real regular, just like yours.

(RADIO smiled at LITTLE BOY. He knew his words came from a good place.)

LITTLE BOY

That must have been a bummer being just like everyone else. Did you at least have that cool boom box back then?

RADIO

Nah my Dad gave me Techtonic after I got out of the hospital.

LITTLE BOY

The hospital? What were you doing there?

RADIO

My Mom, my Dad, and I were in a pretty bad car accident almost six months ago. We were all in the same hospital at the same time. Things were so crazy back then.

LITTLE BOY

Oh, the accident. Is that where you got your super voice?

RADIO

In a round-about way I guess you could say that's where I found out I had it.

LITTLE BOY

Did your Dad get superpowers too?

RADIO

Yeahhhhh, he did, he ended up with a magic leg.

LITTLE BOY

Get out! What can he do with it? Can he kick through doors? What about jumping over fences? Is he faster than the Juice?

RADIO

We're not quite sure what he can do with it. He hasn't used it yet. I hope he does one day.

LITTLE BOY

Whew. I bet you do. It's probably loaded with all kinds of gadgets.

RADIO

No, not this model. It's pretty basic. It's just taking him time to get used to a lot of things after the accident. It's like everything changed in the blink of an eye.

LITTLE BOY

It must be a prototype. I read about prototypes in my comic books. Man, two superheroes in one family. (LITTLE BOY'S voice rose in intensity and pitch.) That's crazy Radio.

RADIO

I KNOW!

(They laughed together again.)

LITTLE BOY

I gotta meet him, Radio.

RADIO

No, you got that backwards. He's gotta meet you Little Man.

LITTLE BOY

Me? No way. There's nothing special about me Radio.

RADIO

Yes, you Little Man. You're just the spark he needs right now.

LITTLE BOY

Whoa sparks. I got sparks and you can see them? You really think I have Superpowers Radio?

RADIO

Without a doubt. Everyone knows about those hands of yours. You got your own thing, a style no one can copy and an imagination that's out of this world.

LITTLE BOY

What are you talking about Radio?

RADIO

The old heads whisper among themselves and they say you're going to be one of the best to do it one day. They all believe you're going to put the Queen City back on the map.

LITTLE BOY

They do? What's an old head? On what map?

RADIO

Yes. Let me try to explain it. You're a blues man, right? An Old head is someone who's lived long enough to have heard Miles Davis play in person.

LITTLE BOY

Who is Miles Davis? Is he good?

RADIO

Just a little. (RADIO brought his index finger and thumb together real tight.)

LITTLE BOY

And they think I'm going to be like him?

(RADIO smiled and nodded.)

RADIO

Yo Little Man, I also heard you create songs for people. You know every superhero needs a theme song. Right?

LITTLE BOY

Oh snap. You want me to play one for you and your Dad?

RADIO

No just one. We're a team.

LITTLE BOY

A dynamic duo. Like Batman and Robin.

RADIO

Nah just father and son. The best duo ever.

LITTLE BOY

(Ouch. That left a little sting.) Oh, fathers and sons. What are their superpowers?

RADIO

The most powerful of them all. Love. A Father can change the world for his son and a son can change the world for his father with the words they share.

LITTLE BOY

Ohhhhhh. Words. Nice. I get that. When they talk about their enemy's powers they can fight better. What's your Dad's super-hero name?

RADIO

He doesn't have one yet. You got the gift, why don't you give him one?

LITTLE BOY

For real. OK. Hmmm, if I had a bionic leg, I'd call myself Hydraulic.

RADIO

I like that. I know he will like it too. Man, he's got a long way to go but a spirit like yours can really get him going.

LITTLE BOY

You mean it ain't easy being a Superhero?

RADIO

I wish it were Little Man. You read the comics. Has it ever been easy being a superhero?

LITTLE BOY

No. It hasn't.

RADIO

Listen, my Dad has had some major setbacks. But you just might get him going. You know, make him want to get back in the fight.

LITTLE BOY

You mean he doesn't want to use his powers?

RADIO

My Dad got hurt pretty bad Little Man. Everything is different now. It's not just him. What hurts him the most is he really misses my Mom and not even I can do anything to change that.

LITTLE BOY

She left? Why? Where did she go?

RADIO

She didn't make it Little Man. She died in the emergency room the night of the accident.

LITTLE BOY

That's so sad. Dag, it's never easy being a superhero.

RADIO

If it were, we'd have a whole lot more of them. Seems to me that all superheroes have to go through some pain before they discover their true purpose.

LITTLE BOY

Why?

RADIO

I don't know why. The thought just came to me while you were talking. I never realized just how much I missed my Mom. It's like I pushed it deep down so I could help my Dad. We never really talk about her.

LITTLE BOY

Why'd you stop?

RADIO

My Mom was gone, my Dad was crushed, and I could barely speak. It was a lot to deal with. And every time I opened my mouth to speak, all I could feel were people's eyes on me. Sometimes I could only see them laughing.

LITTLE BOY

Are you sure they weren't smiling?

RADIO

You know what Little Man. I don't know. My doctor said I was in shock back then. Before meeting you, I would have said I'm pretty sure they were laughing at me. Now, I'm not so sure. Maybe they were just trying to help me. Maybe they were just as amazing as you.

LITTLE BOY

You know what Radio? My Uncle Benny has this story he calls paths. He said the Good Lord can see every path we could ever walk down and everything that could ever happen to us on each of those paths, at the same time.

RADIO

So, what do you think he meant by that?

LITTLE BOY

I don't know. I couldn't figure it out. So, I finally asked him, and he explained it to me. He said that all paths lead us back to the One. Then he said, there are paths where we learn lessons that are only meant for us, and there are other paths where we're part of lessons that are meant for people that we may or may not know.

RADIO

Man, how old are you???

LITTLE BOY

Twelve.

RADIO

More like twelve hundred. (Shaking his head emphatically.) There isn't another twelve-year-old on this Earth who thinks like you.

(LITTLE BOY laughed again. It felt even better this time. Maybe RADIO was right. He did have powers. Maybe he was a superhero.)

RADIO

I made that tape for you because a little bird told me you were missing someone.

LITTLE BOY

Was this a New Orleans bird?

RADIO

I don't know. Who could know such a thing?

(LITTLE BOY rolled his eyes towards the Heavens. Only one other person spoke like that.)

LITTLE BOY

Lisaaaaaa. (In a barely audible tone.)

RADIO

Maybe I made it for me too. It felt good making it. It felt even better giving it to you. Seeing that smile on your face made me feel alive for the first time in a long time.

LITTLE BOY

Maybe someone made you do it so we could finally meet?

RADIO

He works in mysterious ways.

LITTLE BOY

Maybe your Dad needs to receive a special message too.

RADIO

You might be on to something. We both kind of crawled into our own shell.

LITTLE BOY

Let's call him.

RADIO

Right now?

LITTLE BOY

Why not?

It was an unusual request, but this was an unusual day. Two kids from opposite sides of the tracks had become one. They walked together to a payphone near the bus stop. RADIO dialed the number to his father's hospital room.

RADIO'S DAD

Hey son, you, OK? Is everything alright?

(RADIO had never dialed the number during the day.)

RADIO

Dad, I'm fine. No, I'm better than that, I'm super-duper fine.

(RADIO's DAD heard a sound he hadn't heard from RADIO in a long time. It sounded like happiness.)

RADIO

Dad, I have someone I need you to talk to. His name is Little Boy, but I call him Little Man. He's special Dad. Miles Davis special. Can you say hi to him for me?

RADIO'S DAD

Yes, please hand him the phone.

(RADIO handed the receiver to LITTLE BOY.)

RADIO'S DAD

Hey Little Man, how you doing?

LITTLE BOY

I'm fine, Sir. How are you doing today?

RADIO'S DAD

I'm good I suppose. I have my ups and downs like everyone else.

LITTLE BOY

Well, we're going to make today one of your best days ever. Radio told me all about your bionic leg. I know new technology can be hard to get used to. But we need you to try it out, so you can get out here and start saving this world again. The whole world has been waiting on you Hydraulic. That's your superhero name. Just so you know. That's what the people will call you. I hope you like it. You can change it if you don't. My feelings won't be hurt. Maybe a little. But its still cool.

(RADIO knew his Dad was laughing on the other end of the line.)

LITTLE BOY

Radio he won't stop laughing.

RADIO'S DAD

You are a special young man. Do you have any other orders for me?

LITTLE BOY

No. I just want you to know how special you are. The world needs you to get up now. There are many who need to see you on your feet so that they can get back on theirs. Your story is part of your superpower. Your story is going to give them so much strength, and power. Do you believe me?

RADIO's DAD

Sir yes Sir. Hydraulic is officially reporting for duty.

LITTLE BOY

Ah that's a Sir sandwich Sir. I get it now Otis. (OTIS would have laughed if he were there.) Thanks, Mr. Hydraulic. The world anxiously awaits your first day on the job

(LITTLE BOY excitedly handed the receiver to RADIO.)

RADIO

Hey Dad, Little Man's working on a theme song for us. It appears that I'm a superhero too. He's out of this world with this guitar. Yo Little Man, what's my superhero name?

LITTLE BOY

It's Voice Magic.

RADIO

That's fly. Did you hear that, Dad? My superhero name is Voice Magic.

RADIO'S DAD

Yeah, that's cool. Ask him to play a few bars from our theme song.

RADIO

Little Man can you play a little for my Dad?

LITTLE BOY

You know it. Anything for Hydraulic and Voice Magic.
LITTLE BOY put on his sunglasses and pulled out a tie and tied it around his curly afro. Like all superheroes he too needed a disguise to protect his identity.

Taking the guitar from his back he played the beginning of the song the three of them would share for the remainder of their days.

RADIO

You should see him, Dad. The boy has style. He's fierce with it isn't he Dad?

(LITTLE BOY had transformed into his alter-ego Legend.)

RADIO'S DAD

Yeah, he's real with it. Voice Magic, my physical therapist is here, and Hydraulic has some real work to do today. If you know what I mean. We'll talk later, OK? Make sure you bring that Little Man by the house when I get out of here. I've got to meet him face-to-face. Thanks for the call. I really needed that. It felt so good to talk to you. I know I haven't spoken many words to you lately, just know that you are my everything and I love you so much. I'm sorry it took me so long to say it.

(RADIO's DAD struggled to say it all without crying.)

RADIO

I love you too Dad. (As he too wiped tears from his eyes.)

LITTLE BOY

(LITTLE BOY shouted.) Goodbye Mister Hydraulic.

RADIO'S DAD

Tell him I'll see him soon.

RADIO

Alright Dad. I will. I'll see you later. (He hung up the receiver.) Little Man that was really cool. My Dad hasn't sounded like that in a long, long, time. He can't wait to meet you.

LITTLE BOY

That's amazing. I'm a sidekick to two superheroes. I can't wait to tell this story to my Uncle Benny.

RADIO

Yo, you're going to tell a story to a storyteller. Now that's the real story.

LITTLE BOY rubbed his chin thinking about the implications of telling this story to the greatest storyteller he knew, his Uncle Benny.

Noticing that his bus was approaching in the distance, LITTLE BOY took off his tie and sunglasses and put them in his pocket. Voice Magic and Legend pounded fists and hugged, then LITTLE BOY made his way across the tracks.

(SPOTLIGHT ON RADIO DANCING)

(THEME SONG PLAYING IN THE BACKGROUND

(BLACK OUT)

(END OF SCENE)

(END OF ACT)

ACT 2

Scene 1
Mika

SETTING: Six months earlier.

MIKA was, is, and will always be LITTLE BOY's very own personal guardian angel. Today was a day that had been ordained before the creation of the world. A day for her to deliver a most important message to the little boy, who from time to time, could get so lost in his blues.

It was a timeless message, one meant for yesterday, today, and tomorrow. A message LITTLE BOY could tuck deep down inside himself to recall whenever he needed to hear it the most.

That's just the way MIKA spoke her truth. Always operating on multiple levels, her words penetrated every part of your soul. Going backwards, flying forward, and at times just hovering right there in front of you, daring you to ignore them.

Today she had sent an urgent message through REVERAND, requesting LITTLE BOY's presence immediately. This was a most unusual request. Time had never been that big of a deal between them. They didn't see time like that. When they were together time stopped.

What could be so important when the fun began whenever their footsteps found one another? Today, time was going to make his presence felt.

LITTLE BOY arrived early dressed in his finest. MIKA was a Queen, and you didn't visit Queens dressed in your play clothes. It was his only suit, an Easter special, a few years old, it was his favorite color, sky blue and polyester.

LITTLE BOY was quite the sight, the afro, the suit, the platform Stacy Adams, and the guitar strapped over his back.

MIKA told him the suit looked good on him the first time he wore it and that was all LITTLE BOY would ever need to hear on the matter.

He had taken his time walking to the hospital. Stopping along the way to find the roses that OTIS had told him to always keep his eyes peeled for.

They represented the hidden treasures that are all around us. With each rose he discovered; LITTLE BOY's understanding of OTIS' message increased.

At RISE: Exiting the elevator LITTLE BOY made his way down the hall towards MIKA's room. As he made the turn to enter her room, his countenance changed instantly, the room was full of sad faces. It was as if he had walked into the eye of a storm. A room raining tears.

Before he could enter the room, REVEREND pulled him aside and tried his best to show LITTLE BOY that despite the rain showers, the sun was still in the room.

LITTLE BOY was scared for the first time since he had known of the illness that was Mika's. He watched without emotion as each member of MIKA's family kissed her on the forehead. Each one clutching her hand and whispering words he could not make out.

When they finished their last words, they slowly made their way out of the room, walking as if in a trance. Each stopping at LITTLE BOY, for a moment temporarily snapping out of the sad reality, to hug MIKA's favorite person in the whole wide world, the LITTLE BOY dressed in the Blues. Irony. Yes.

Looking into their eyes LITTLE BOY found himself lost for a moment in their storm clouds.

REVEREND was the last one to leave the room. He was drained but found the reserve he needed for LITTLE BOY.

REVERAND

Little Boy come with me for a moment. Mika's going to a need a minute to get ready for you. She's real tired right now. I'm pretty sure if she felt she had the time she would have asked you to come another day. But she doesn't have that kind of time anymore.

LITTLE BOY did not understand the meaning of this. In his mind if she didn't feel well, she should have told him to wait until she felt better. As REVEREND looked down at LITTLE BOY, he could see the confusion written all over his face, noting how his tiny hands had tightened into little fists, his heart pounding, while raindrops formed at the corners of his big brown eyes. The roses fell to the floor in a heap. This is what fear looks like. LITTLE BOY was scared.

REVEREND

Walk with me son. Let's sit down right over here.

REVEREND motioned with his hand towards a couple of chairs sitting outside of MIKA's room. LITTLE BOY approached them with REVEREND, but instead of sitting, he began to pace back and forth in front of them, as was his way whenever he was scared.

LITTLE BOY

Reverend my feet won't let me sit down. I don't understand what's happening. What do you mean Mika doesn't have time anymore? That's Mika in there, she's ten, and she's the fastest and most powerful girl in the world. Everybody knows that. What's really going on? What happened to all the wires and where are the machines that were taking care of her? The ones that were tracking her power. She was getting better, right? Everyone told me she was getting better. Didn't they tell you the same thing? I just saw her the other day.

REVEREND

Little Boy. I know it seems like it was yesterday, but that was three months ago. That was the last time she saw anyone here. Don't you remember seeing me? We were here together.

LITTLE BOY

Yes.

REVEREND

Back then we all thought she was getting better. This has caught everyone off guard. Even the doctors. Please sit-down son. You're making me nervous. Can you do that for me?

LITTLE BOY

I wish I could, but my feet won't let me. I'm afraid if I stop walking, I just might explode, because I feel like screaming Reverend. This can't be happening. I want to know what's going on. I want the truth this time. I want to know why everyone left her. Shouldn't they be here praying even more? Maybe we're saying all the wrong words to the Lord? Maybe it's us and not her. Maybe we're messing this up. He can save her if we ask Him, right? He's the Lord. Why else wouldn't he save Mika Reverend? We've all been praying to him. We all love her. I know He loves her too.

(Reverend comforted LITTLE BOY and waited patiently as he got his words out to the universe.)

LITTLE BOY

Maybe it's my fault? I could have come to see her more often. Maybe the Lord thought I stopped caring. Maybe He knows I stopped praying every day. Reverend I didn't know I had to keep asking for the same thing over and over. I thought she was getting better. So, I stopped. I thought my prayers had been answered. I don't understand what's going on here. Do we need a miracle now? Doesn't He know the fair is next month? Mika and I have big plans for the fair. We always do. We've never missed the fair. It's always been me and Mika at the fair. Everyone knows that. Doesn't the Lord know that too? If Mika's not with me, who am I supposed to go to the fair with?

RERVEREND

Little Boy, I know Mika is your best friend in the world. Tell me this much, did she somehow stop being your best friend just because you couldn't see her every day like you used to?
(LITTLE BOY shook his head slowly in response to the question.)

REVEREND

No, that didn't happen, in fact the two of you became even closer. We all witnessed that and that made us all feel a little better, even if it was just for a moment. Looking at you two together was like looking into Heaven. That little girl in there is always going to be your best friend. You didn't do anything wrong; we didn't do anything wrong; Mika didn't do anything wrong, and neither did the Lord. She's just sick and her bodies not getting well. We all know she's as strong as a lion cub. She has fought so hard for so long and we all know she would never stop fighting, because she fights for more than herself. But this disease, this cancer, it doesn't stop fighting either. And it doesn't fight fair. It attacks her even while she's sleeping. Can you imagine that kind of fight, Little Boy?

LITTLE BOY

No. (Wiping the tears away from his eyes.)

REVEREND

We can't see it because it's deep inside of her, but the Lord sees this struggle and I believe He has let her know that she doesn't have to fight anymore. He has comforted her mind and her heart. She knows He will take care of the one's she's leaving behind. She doesn't have anything left to prove, and even though the Lord has told her this, she still needs to hear it from us. She cares so much. That's the Mika we all know.

LITTLE BOY

Why did she tell me to come here today?

REVEREND

Mika needs you to tell her that you're going to be OK without her. She needs you to promise her that you'll do everything in your power to see her again on the other side. She needs to know that you'll get out of here and see the world and let the world see you too. Look, you did the hard part and took the most crucial step. You came when she called. She'll always remember that when she needed you the most you came to her. Nothing will ever change that fact. And what is more important than that? Nothing. Some people will live their whole life and never experience that. They will never know that they were the most important thing in the world to another soul. Mika got her answer at ten. You were her everything. You got to praise the Lord for that.

(LITTLE BOY nodded and cracked a half-smile, it was the first step in what would be a long, long, winter.)

REVEREND

Now all you have to do is be you. Leave her a part of you. Something she can take with her, something she can tuck deep down inside where no one can get to it. I pray that you understand. She told me you would.

LITTLE BOY

I do.

REVEREND

Good, that's why you're here today. You're the last person she's going to talk to. Now go over there and pick up those beautiful roses and let her know how you feel about her. You know she loves flowers. I'm pretty sure she has something to tell you too. Something that she could only tell you face-to-face. But first you gotta fix your face.

(REVEREND handed LITTLE BOY a handkerchief and he wiped his face with it. When he was done REVEREND told him to keep it. Just in case he needed it again.)

REVEREND

Listen up, Mika has seen and heard enough sadness today. What she needs now is to see the one face that has always made her smile. That's what the Lord needs you to do for Him. He wants you to walk her to the gate. Now go on in there. The two of you have some unfinished business.

LITTLE BOY

Business?

REVEREND

Yes business. A few things to talk through.

LITTLE BOY

Ohhhhh yeahhhh. The fair. Yeah, we gotta talk about that for sure.

REVEREND

That's as good a place to start as any. Where it goes from there is totally up to you.

LITTLE BOY

Reverend thank you for staying back with me.

REVEREND

You don't have to thank me Little Boy. This is what I was born to do. The truth is, I needed you more than you needed me today.

You two are something special. Real treasures. Because of you two we got to experience so many miracles. But I gotta go now. I'll see you soon, OK? If you need to call me later, here's my number.

LITTLE BOY

Thanks Reverend. I'll be OK. I'll see you at church.

They hugged, then REVEREND departed, and LITTLE BOY finally entered MIKA'S room. It was cold, but it smelled pretty. There were flowers of every type, and they were everywhere. There were rose petals of all colors all over MIKA's bed. She was in Heaven.

LITTLE BOY

Girl, what are you still doing in this bed? Don't you know the fair is next week? You know everyone's asking me about you. Even the new Korean kid. They're all planning what they're going to wear to the fair, but they won't pick out anything until they find out what you're going to wear first. Which means they ask me the same questions every single day. What is Mika wearing Little Boy? Its driving me crazy. What am I supposed to tell them? They all know you're the talker of this group. You know I hate talking. Yet because of you I still stop and have the same discussion every time they corner me. One question leads to another and then they want to talk to me about myself. Uhhhhhhhh. It's like I somehow became you. But I'm not you Mika. I don't like people like you do. I only like talking to you.

MIKA

Well, it appears that you, Little Boy, have gotten yourself into quite the pickle.

LITTLE BOY

A pickle? What are you talking about Mika?

MIKA

It's a figure of speech that my Nana uses. Let's call it a situation. Something you never saw coming. An unforeseen event.

LITTLE BOY

If that's a pickle? Then call me a pickle.

(MIKA laughed even though it made her hurt. LITTLE BOY knew she would.)

MIKA

You're so crazy. But you gotta stop with the jokes. It hurts when I laugh. I heard you talking to Reverend. If I'm going to make it to the fair, I'm afraid it's going to be inside of you. So, what are you gonna do about that?

(LITTLE BOY sat staring, head cocked to the side, waiting for MIKA's explanation. She almost missed the cue.)

MIKA

Are you going to crawl back inside that guitar? Go back to being a loner? Cut off all our friends? I hope not. You love the fair Little Boy. Other than playing that guitar in the park, it's the only other place I've ever seen you happy. Am I right or wrong?

LITTLE BOY

You're right. I love the fair when we're there together.

MIKA

Well, if you love the fair like you like me, you gotta do this for me, you gotta do this for them, and most importantly you gotta do this for yourself. It's not as hard as it looks. Start with the kicks. Keep it simple, none of us has a lot of money. Pretty much everyone can afford blue strings, blue t-shirts, and black shorts and if they can't there are things you can all do to raise the money you need. I showed you these things. Last thing they need, afros looking fly with their fists in the sky. Do that part for me. So that they know that I'm always with them. You can do this Little Boy because the Lord made you special. You're a natural leader. You always will be. You just have to let the world see how special He made you.

LITTLE BOY

But what if they don't listen to me?

MIKA

I already thought about that. Look over there on that stand. I wrote them a note. A simple message. It says, "Do what Little Boy says or else." Then I signed it. Trust me, that's all you're going to need. LITTLE BOY couldn't help but laugh as he looked at the note. At the bottom of the note, there was a drawing of a face with x's for eyes, with the words "your face" written underneath it, and to the right of it a huge boxing glove with the words "MIKA" written inside of it. It was classic Mika motivation.

LITTLE BOY

Are you ever going to go to the fair with me again?

MIKA

Yes, but not like you think. I'm sick and I'm tired but I'm going to try to explain it to you. Have you ever played Ms. Pac Man?

LITTLE BOY

The video game?

MIKA

Nahhhhh the board game Little Boy. Of course, the video game. Geez. Sometimes you make my head hurt.

LITTLE BOY

Yeah, I played the game before. (With a big cheesy smile.)

MIKA

Anyway, that game is like my body. Except inside my body there are way more ghost than Ms. Pac Man has to fight. And no matter how hard I fight they always win because every time I gobble up one, ten more ghosts appear. There's just too many of them. I have learned through this sickness, that there are some games you just can't win. Everyone plays this game called life. My game just ended early. Little Boy, I am so tired, and when I try to rest, the ghosts fight even harder.

LITTLE BOY

That's so unfair.

MIKA

Yeah, that not nice. (She chuckled at their little inside joke.) I know it isn't fair and I wish I had better news for you, but I don't.

You're my best friend and we have had some of the greatest adventures ever. I know we have so many more ahead of us. Just not here. Not like this. One day you'll understand what I mean.

LITTLE BOY

We have had so much fun Mika. But if not here and not now, then when will we have our next adventure?

MIKA

Little Boy, if you love the Lord with all your heart and soul and you treat people like He treats you, we'll see each other again and when we do, we'll have adventures you can't even imagine. Like one where you chase me and actually catch me. Perhaps even better than that.

LITTLE BOY

I was that close to catching you, Mika. (LITTLE BOY held his thumb and forefinger about an inch apart.)

MIKA

I know you thought you'd catch me one day. But I bet you didn't think it would be today. I know I didn't. That's why it's so funny to me. It's downright hilarious.
(MIKA laughed and coughed a little, and LITTLE BOY was there to hold her.)

LITTLE BOY

What's so funny about that Mika?

MIKA

It's kind of like Charlie Brown finally kicking the ball but only because Peppermint Patty got her shots and couldn't lift her arms.

LITTLE BOY

Oh, it's like that. You still got jokes. (LITTLE BOY laughed like the good ole days.) I'm not that slow you know. I've gotten a lot faster.

MIKA

Of course, you did, you were chasing the wind. You had no choice but to get faster.

LITTLE BOY

I almost caught you once, remember?

MIKA

When? Are you still talking about the time I came home from church and still had on my Sunday shoes? Little Boy, I wouldn't tell anyone that story if I were you.

LITTLE BOY

It did happen.

MIKA

I slipped and fell, and you still couldn't catch me. Like I said I wouldn't tell that story to anyone.

LITTLE BOY

Maybe you wouldn't. But when I tell everyone the story of how I almost caught the wind, they won't need to know she was wearing a purple dress and Sunday shoes.

MIKA

Ahhhh, you remembered. So, you're a storyteller now. Pretty good at it I see. You are a boy of many talents. Lawd, Lawd, Lawd, what I wouldn't give to be here to see you share them with the world.

LITTLE BOY

Where are you going? Home?

MIKA

Yeah, you could say that.

LITTLE BOY

What do you mean now, more riddles?

MIKA

Little Boy I'm never going back to my house and I'm never going back to the fair. I'm going to that place where you look for your Dad.

LITTLE BOY

Really?

MIKA

Yes. That's why I had everyone I wanted to see come here today, to say goodbye. That's why I wanted you here and the reason I saved you for last. You're my best friend in the whole wide world. My sun rose and set with you. It's crazy because I've only known you a couple of years. When I first saw you with your guitar and all your silence you were the biggest mystery ever, I never knew you until you spoke to me. You said, "Hi my name is Little Boy and we're going to be best friends." It's funny to me now, how the words of someone who spoke so few of them could mean so much to me. I never imagined we would be this close. You know with you being all grumpy and stuffy all the time. Just look at you, you ole grumpy old man. (She pinched his cheeks like his grandma. She knew he would protest.) But I know that's your shield. It almost scared me away in the beginning. But you were so interesting that I knew I had to take the time to figure you out. You were just so amazing to me. (MIKA held his face and looked deep into his eyes.)

LITTLE BOY

Oh, so you got me figured out now. Like one of your riddles. (LITTLE BOY laughed so he didn't cry.)

MIKA

We're all riddles Little Boy. Don't trip on that. You're more than that to me. With you, it's your heart. It is just so biggggg that I get scared for you sometimes. I know you feel everything all the time. In the beginning, it was hard to figure out when things had begun to become too much for you. I was so worried that no one would be here to catch you when that happened again. But I know the Lord has made special people for you who will fight through all that grumpiness and they're going to have your back and you'll know them the moment they walk into your life. Do you believe me? I say them because you're going to need a village to keep you here.

LITTLE BOY

Yeah, I think you're right. You're always right.

MIKA

Very well. Now that that's settled. On to the deeper things. I'm so glad I met you. It was like God opened my diary and found my secret wish list for a best friend and sent you to me just in time. When I meet him, I'm going to talk to him about those rough edges of yours though.

LITTLE BOY

Girl I ain't got no rough edges. (As he shaped his perfect afro.)

MIKA

You don't now. We smoothed them out and polished you up, so you could see your shine. Now look at you. You're amazing. But listen closely. Don't ever go back to being the old you. Even when it seems like it's easier. I want you to promise me that you won't. Promise me.

LITTLE BOY

I promise you.

MIKA

Pinky swear?

LITTLE BOY

Pinky swear.

(They did that thing they did with their pinky fingers and a promise that couldn't be broken had been made.)

MIKA

Good. You have been blessed with many talents, and if you use them, He's going to take you around the world. You just have to believe. Do you believe?

LITTLE BOY

I do.

MIKA

Do you believe in Him?

LITTLE BOY

Yes, with all my heart and all my soul. You know this.

MIKA

Just checking. Man, I've been doing all the talking as usual. But I called you here, so I could hear your voice one last time.

LITTLE BOY

You know how I am with the words Mika. I keep it short and simple. I love you. There, I said it. I have since the first day you ran by me. I was so amazed at how fast you were. Watching you run was crazy. No one could catch you. Chasing you was like chasing the wind. Even though I knew I couldn't catch you, I learned to love running because of you, and running made it easier for me to think, it calmed me down. You gave me that gift and I asked myself. Who could know such things? Who could know what another person needed without being told? You taught me so much by your words, but you did more than just talk. You showed me how to daydream and the nightmares went away. I thought we would be running like this for the rest of our lives and I'm afraid of being here without you. Actually, I'm scared Mika. You brought out the best in me and you're leaving, and I don't know if I can be me without you.

(LITTLE BOY couldn't hold it anymore. He rained tears.)

MIKA

Little Boy I'll always be with you. I'm in your heart and in your mind. You don't have to look for me. I'll always be with you. All you have to do is remember me. Keep going to the fair. Get closer to our friends. Lead them. Talk about me every now and then to keep me alive in them too. Then open your heart and mind to them like you did to me. I promise if you do all these things, you'll never forget me. Whew, I'm really tired now and I need you to go to the nurse's desk and tell them to send my grandparents back up. Can you do that for me?

LITTLE BOY

Yes. (Sniffling.) Do you want me to come back up?

MIKA

No.

LITTLE BOY

OK. This is it. I love you. I really, really, love you.

MIKA

If you really love me leave right now and please don't look back OK. Promise me you won't look back. Please go now.

                    LITTLE BOY

I promise. Until I see you again.

LITTLE BOY stood up from the bed and leaned over and kissed Mika on the lips. It was their first and last kiss and she rubbed it off, just like he knew she would, and they laughed and cried, as they stared into each other's souls, lost for a moment, unable to blink, until MIKA nudged him towards the door. It was the last time he would ever see her alive.

(As LITTLE BOY walked towards the door MIKA took a deep breath and passed. He didn't look back. She didn't want him to see her leave. He had promised. They NEVER broke a promise they made to one another.)

                    (BLACKOUT)

                   (END OF SCENE)

ACT 2

Scene 2
Ninja

SETTING: It was almost noon on the Soul Train line and people all over the world, one in particular, were impatiently awaiting its arrival.

It was filled with dancers who possessed all the latest moves and grooves that when learned would separate those who could from those who could not.

LITTLE BOY and SISTER GIRL were two of those who could. LITTLE BOY waited impatiently for his big little sister. Although smaller in stature she had been his protector from the womb.

The same one who showed him how to tie his shoes was the only one who would ball up her fists without hesitation if anyone threatened to hurt him.

They never boarded the train at the same time. She would make it downstairs to the station in her due time, but only after LITTLE BOY nagged her until he had worked himself into a frenzy. It was a strange routine; one they had choreographed so many Soul Train days ago.

LITTLE BOY nick-named her the Quiet Storm because when she danced, no matter how loud the music was, the whole atmosphere changed, and it got quiet. She commanded attention.

To a normal kid this could be most unnerving but LITTLE BOY loved silence and when they danced together, he simply focused on doing his best to keep up. Like chasing the wind, he called MIKA, dancing in a quiet storm, only made him better. This was their bond. This was the gift that SISTER GIRL had given to him. The freedom he found in his love of expression through dance. LITTLE BOY was a B-Boy.

At RISE: LITTLE BOY turned on the small black and white television set that sat on top of the large color console that didn't work, in the living room.

The TV sculptures was a common accent piece in many of the homes in his neighborhood. Was it art deco? Who could tell? What child could know such things?

It was an eclectic piece of sculpture that no one ever stopped to stare at or conversate over. It was just one of those things. LITTLE BOY grew up believing that all Black people collected broken TV's. It's just what they did.

LITTLE BOY used an old pair of pliers to change the channel. Then he took a smaller pair of needle nose pliers to turn the knob with the small numbers to channel 29 or 78 or whichever low budget channel carried his beloved Soul Train.

Many years ago, he inherited the thankless task of setting the rabbit ears for the best possible reception. This was no exact science and over time he learned how to bribe LITTLE BROTHER with just enough penny candy to make him forget he was being hustled. This part was an exact science. He had learned that everyone had a price.

LITTLE BOY
(LITTLE BOY shouts upstairs.) Sister Girl hurry up. It's about to come on.

SISTER GIRL
Hold your horse's boy. I'll be down in a minute. You act like this is every week. What is wrong with you? (Shaking her head and laughing out loud.)

LITTLE BOY
But you're going to miss the beginning. That's the best part.

SISTER GIRL
Not for me. It's a dancing train.

LITTLE BOY

You used to like it.

(Then speaking to the choir.)

LITTLE BOY

Why do we have to do this every week? I don't know why she acts like she doesn't care when I know she does. Now she don't like the train no more, but she dances just like the train, and acts like she hates the song, when she sings all the words. (Looking upstairs.) Oooh, you make me sick sometimes. (With his little hand balled up into a fist towards her room.)

SISTER GIRL

What did you say?

LITTLE BOY

I said stop playing you know what today is about.

SISTER GIRL

It sounded like you said you want me to come down there and make you scream and shout?

LITTLE BOY

No, I said I'm ready to come up there and punch you in the mouth. (LITTLE BOY spoke these words in a very hushed tone.)

SISTER GIRL

I know it didn't say what I thought I heard. Because I know you didn't say anything about punching me in the mouth. Did you Little Boy?

(Crickets.)

SISTER GIRL

Did you???

LITTLE BOY

No!

SISTER GIRL

No what?

LITTLE BOY

No Number One Soul Sista.

(LITTLE BOY hated this arrangement. A bet gone wrong.)

SISTER GIRL

That's what I thought.

LITTLE BOY

(Speaking again to the choir in an even lower tone.) She does this every Saturday. Why do I keep falling for the okie-doke? One of these days I'm going to get her good. Maybe I won't call her down and then I'll learn all the new moves by myself and when we go the next party, I'll be looking fly and she'll be looking whickety whack. Then she'll act right. Uhm hmm. Yep. I'll show her.

SISTER GIRL

You do know I can hear every word you're mumbling down there through my vent.

LITTLE BOY

(LITTLE BOY noticed the vents for the very first time ever. They had lived there twelve months.) I didn't say anything.

SISTER GIRL

I know you didn't. Now don't call me when Soul Train comes on and see what happens.

Was this an actual request? Was she telling him not to tell her? When SISTER GIRL spoke like this LITTLE BOY was so confused. He was so literal.

LITTLE BOY

I'm not scared of you girl. (Mumbled in a low tone.)

SISTER GIRL

Why are you whispering?

LITTLE BOY

I'm not whispering.

LITTLE BOY pretended to shadow box with his imaginary sister. Throwing flurries and dancing around her like Ali as he counted her out. Although a KO would never happen, a little brother could still dream.

SISTER GIRL

You shadow boxing? Make sure your shadow doesn't knock you out again.

(LITTLE BOY heard SISTER GIRL laughing loudly upstairs. LITTLE BROTHER couldn't stop himself from snickering and struggled to remain focused on the mission.)

LITTLE BOY

(LITTLE BOY walked over to the staircase.) It's about to start for real this time.

SISTER GIRL

Yeah, I know Chicken Little.

SISTER GIRL refused to come down until she heard Don Cornelius.

LITTLE BOY

The Soul Train is Coming! The Soul Train is Coming! (As he mimicked the trains moves.)

SISTER GIRL

You can't fool me knucklehead. The Soul Train ain't coming.

LITTLE BOY

Yes, it is.

SISTER GIRL

No, it isn't.

LITTLE BOY

YES, IT IS! (At the top of his lungs.)

SISTER GIRL

No, it's not. (At a whisper that penetrated LITTLE BOY's head like a bull horn.)

LITTLE BOY

(LITTLE BOY had been triggered.) You know what? You're right this time. THE SOUL TRAIN AIN'T COMING!!!

LITTLE BOY had finally had enough and decided today was the day he would take a stand. Today he would become a Little Man. He stomped over to the TV and turned the volume down to a whisper, then picked up his favorite comic book and guitar, and left the house for the park.

He told LITTLE BROTHER if he knew what was best for him, he would continue holding the antenna because when SISTER GIRL came downstairs, she was not going to be happy. It was better this way, only one little brother would have to take an L.

LITTLE BOY knew he wouldn't move if he ponied up enough candy to make it worth his while. Was it a shake-down? No, just family business.

SISTER GIRL

(Running down the stairs.) The Soul Train is Coming! The Soul Train is... OK, where did Little Boy go? (Looking in the direction of LITTLE BROTHER.)

(LITTLE BROTHER armed with a mouth full of candy and both hands on the antenna, tried to use his eyes to direct SISTER GIRL towards the door.)

SISTER GIRL

OK so he went out the door. Where did he go Dobie Gillis?

Answering this question proved to be too difficult for eyes alone. So, LITTLE BROTHER remained frozen in the same position LITTLE BOY had left him in.

SISTER GIRL

Let go of the antenna and swallow the candy.

LITTLE BROTHER acknowledged his predicament and let go of the antenna. He couldn't speak. Swallowing that much candy without chewing it would kill him. It was a catch-22. He would die on his own terms.

SISTER GIRL

Where did he go? (As if talking to a toddler. A style that they would later learn had been coined Barney style.

(LITTLE BROTHER pointed at the door.)

SISTER GIRL

I already know he walked out the door dummy. Where did he go? That was the question. Didn't I tell you to swallow the candy? What's wrong with your mouth?

(LITTLE BROTHER opened his mouth to what appeared to be a fishing net full of candy fish remains.)

SISTER GIRL

You put the whole bag in your mouth? Are you crazy? You do know you're going to choke to death one of these days. Just don't do it today. I'm not trying to hear Mom's mouth and you know we don't do emergency rooms. Did he take his guitar with him? (LITTLE BROTHER nodded.) Did he take anything else? (LITTLE BROTHER rendered his best Spider-Man impersonation.) Is that the dance he learned today? (LITTLE BROTHER shook his head with curiosity.) Is he doing graffiti now? (LITTLE BROTHER shook his head emphatically, wondering to himself, with his clues, how could she be so cold?) OK you really stink at this, and I'll never figure it out so write it down. (LITTLE BROTHER wrote the word Spider-Man.)

SISTER GIRL

OKkkkkkkkkk. Little Brother, you really need to work on your charade skills. (LIITLE BROTHER had the same thought about SISTER GIRL.) Did he take his comic books? (LITTLE BROTHER jumped for joy with two thumbs up.) So, he's not planning on coming back for a while. Thanks, I think. Now get back on that antenna. Mutual of Omaha's Wild Kingdom is about to come on.

(LITTLE BROTHER stood firmly and held out his hand and SISTER GIRL put a penny in it. Today was not the day to press his luck.)

SISTER GIRL

Make it enough.

LITTLE BROTHER did as he was told. There was nothing to be gained from taking a stand. Especially when they both knew he would eventually find her stash and do just as she instructed him. Make it enough.

SISTER GIRL grabbed a bag of chips from the kitchen and her blanket from upstairs and flopped down on the couch waiting for her second favorite TV show.

Out of nowhere and as if shot out of a cannon LITTLE BOY rushed through the front door. He had been crying. His clothes were in disarray, his comic book ripped in half, his guitar missing strings, and his lip fat.

LITTLE BROTHER wasn't sure if he should laugh now or laugh later. So, he stood blinking as SISTER GIRL jumped up from the couch to collect the facts like Kojak.

SISTER GIRL

(Temporarily forgetting she was mad at LITTLE BOY.) Who did this?

In her world there was only one person who could beat up her brother and that person was her. LITTLE BOY continued with his shaken theatrics.

SISTER GIRL

Do you want me to call Mom?

(LITTLE BOY shook his head. This question always brought him out of any of his episodes. No matter the severity.)

SISTER GIRL

What happened?

LITTLE BOY

I was sitting in the park minding my own business. (Sniffles for the full effect.) Just reading my comic book. (More sniffling.) There was a group of boys I didn't know with a boom box, some 40's, and squares. I didn't think anything of it. They were ticking and tocking like scrubs do. Wanna be B-Boys. I wasn't trying to get involved in that. Then Ninja, you know the one who carries the nun-chucks and robs everyone, the one who can't dance a lick. Well, he saw some girls checking out the scrubs and decided to get in on it. You know he looks super old. Like he's thirty or something. He got his old man face at birth. So, these scrubs were scared to tell him no and no one wanted to battle him, because if he won, he was going to beat em up and if he lost, he was going to beat em up worse. So, they had to stand around and watch him do the same ole lame moves he's done forever. But that wasn't enough for him today. There were girls around and he needed a challenger. He needed to beat somebody.

SISTER GIRL

And you were crazy enough to take the challenge?

LITTLE BOY

Hell nah. (They all laughed so loud and so long it was hard for them to catch their breath.) I thought I was invisible. But you know how people like to instigate. They all knew someone was going to get it today. So, they looked at me, and then Ninja saw me. I still wouldn't look up. The whole time I thought my force field would protect me, right up to the moment he snatched my comic book out my hand and ripped it in half. My new edition Spider Man. I was pissed but I still didn't budge. Then he took my guitar and broke one of the strings, then a second, and I knew right then, that he would break them all, if I didn't do something, and then he would move on to me if I didn't get up and dance. So, I stood up.

SISTER GIRL

So, you stood up just to get bet down? Why didn't you run Boy Blunder?

LITTLE BOY

Are you crazy he's faster than Mika?

SISTER GIRL

Why didn't you let him win then?

LITTLE BOY

I tried to. I did my worst moves. I mean the whackest ones I know, and I did them as bad as I could.

SISTER GIRL

Show me one.

(LITTLE BOY did the worst move in his bag.)

SISTER GIRL

Ooohhh yeah that's pretty bad. Soooooooo?

LITTLE BOY

My worst moves were still better than Ninja's best moves. But the crowd wanted blood and they really started making Ninja mad. Shouting, "Little Boy's straight clowning you." So, he ticked-tocked over to me and did this crazy move where he took my head off my shoulders in his hands, then shaped it like an apple, bit into it and spit it out on the ground. Then he placed the bitten apple back on my shoulders. For a second, I must admit I was a little impressed by Ninja's improvisation. Remember this was Ninja. It got him more juice than it should. But remember the crowd wanted to see my blood.

SISTER GIRL

Why didn't you sneak him and take the L right there?

LITTLE BOY

You mean get beat up and lose a battle to the worst dancer in the whole world?

SISTER GIRL

So, you danced and ran home with a fat lip. I hope it was worth it.

LITTLE BOY

Sister Girl, you know how it is with me. I always go right when I should go left. I kept looking at that stupid look on his face and I was like nope not today, Ninja. So, I looked over at the boy with the boom box and handed him my Planet Rock mix tape. Then I put on my shades and tied my tie around my fro in slow motion, so everyone knew right then it was on like Donkey Kong. Ninja was going to get served. The rest, as they say, is history.

SISTER GIRL

Show me how you murdered that Ninja Little Boy. Little Brother cue Planet Rock.

(LITTLE BROTHER located the forty-five and put it on the record player.)

LITTLE BOY hit Ninja with all his signature moves, a combination of mime action, a little moon walk, ticking from his feet to his arms and hands, and then he stepped to Ninja and took his head and passed it from hand to hand and then down to his feet, kicked it up and grabbed it again, flipping it behind his back and proceeded to wipe his butt with it like a rag. At this point SISTER GIRL and LITTLE BROTHER were already on the floor laughing out of control. It was like they were right there with LITTLE BOY watching it all play out. He didn't know it at the time, but he was becoming quite the storyteller.

SISTER GIRL

Please tell me you weren't crazy enough to try to put it back on his shoulders.

LITTLE BOY

No way, I dropped kicked it and tried to use that as a distraction, so I could get away. I grabbed my stuff and took off. I was so hyped I actually thought I could outrun him. For a brief moment I had forgotten about his speed. I knew it was over at the butt wipe. I could see the crazy in his eyes. He caught me, ripped off my tie, stomped on my sunglasses and punched me in the mouth.

SISTER

Was it worth it?

LITTLE BOY

Are you kidding me? I'm a legend now. I'm the only B-Boy in the world that ever battled a Ninja and lived to tell about it. Yeah, I got a fat lip, my glasses broken, and my favorite comic book ripped in half. But I didn't lose. (LITTLE BOY sounded like James Earl Jones.) Not today. I did this for all the real B-Boy's around the world. This is our thing. The Ninja's got their thing. Beating up people and stealing stuff. But this is ours. I had to let him know.

SISTER GIRL

So why you come in here crying?

LITTLE BOY

Because getting punched in the face by a Ninja still hurts. (He felt his face for the first time.)

SISTER GIRL

Would you do it again?

LITTLE BOY

Heck no. I'm running from now on. I'll live to dance another day.

SISTER GIRL

Good because I can't fight your battles anymore. Now that you're battling Ninjas.

LITTLE BOY

I know. Maybe I should take up Kung Fu.

SISTER GIRL

Boy we ain't got no Kung Fu money, you better stick to running. (They all laughed.)

LITTLE BROTHER

Little Boy, tell the story one more time? Pleaseeeeeeee...

LITTLE BOY

You got it. Yo DJ play my song.

With that DJ Lil Brother moved over to the ones and twos and cued the music that would fuel a story they would laugh at for the next forty years, and on that day they had the time of their life, watching and listening to LITTLE BOY act out the scenes to the most improbable story of a LITTLE B-Boy who battled a Ninja and lived to tell about it.

(BLACKOUT)

(END OF SCENE)

ACT 2

Scene 3

Brooklyn

SETTING: It was lunch time on his dial and LITTLE BOY was standing alone in the corner of his second favorite place on Earth. The R&B section at Record Theater. His Heaven on EARTH.

It was an all-inclusive hotspot long before the term had ever been considered. The music you could discover there was amazing and once you became a regular the eclectic staff there taught you how to find its hidden gems.

But the real treasures were the art pieces you found in the crowd. Each a new work of art. LITTLE BOY's favorite piece was on display today. She wasn't the oldest piece there. But she was older than LITTLE BOY and that alone fascinated him.

She worked the afternoon shift every Tuesday – Friday and in just over six months she and Record Theater had become synonymous with one another. She was blessed with the most infectious spirit

LITTLE BOY was intrigued by her the moment he heard her voice. She sang when she spoke. At least that's how LITTLE BOY experienced her. Amazing thing about her, she knew the name and artist on every piece of vinyl in the place.

She was cute as a button. A term LITTLE BOY had been called by an elderly woman who had managed to bring him close enough to pinch his cheeks. Her words didn't make sense back then, but they made absolute sense when he found his eyes fixed on hers. He would later learn that the correct words to describe her were drop dead gorgeous.

LITTLE BOY had heard others call her Shorty. It was cute but it didn't fit his favorite piece of art. She was much more than that. She wasn't from around these parts. A blind man could see that.

She hailed from someplace else. The borough of Brooklyn to be specific. New York City, USA. It could have been France as far as LITTLE BOY was concerned. His world consisted of the four street boundaries of the Gardens. The sticks to a New Yorker. A place filled with single mom's and children without fathers.

Brooklyn was different. That's what LITTLE BOY called her. She brought her own spice to the world. They were a match made in Heaven. At least that's how LITTLE BOY saw the matter.

The reality of the matter was LITTLE BOY had never spoken her name. At least not out loud.

Her hair was pretty. Always perfect. Never the same style three days in a row. Her clothes were right out of the black movies of the day. She was a real superstar. A cool breeze on a hot summer day.

The old heads gawked and crooned when she walked. LITTLE BOY had no idea what that all meant. All he knew was that when he was around her, he felt all warm inside.

At RISE: LITTLE BOY is in the new releases section of the store looking for the Jackson 5's Who's Loving You album. He had to have it. His cheap cassette player had done what it was famous for. Eaten another cassette tape.

BROOKLYN

Can I help you, Romeo?

LITTLE BOY looked up with a very puzzled look on his face. No one had ever called him that before. There had to be a story behind this name.

LITTLE BOY

I'm looking for Who's Loving You by the Jackson 5.

BROOKLYN

The Single or the LP?

LITTLE BOY

Huh?

BROOKLYN

Do you want the single or the LP? (Holding a forty-five and an album in each hand.)

LITTLE BOY

I don't know.

BROOKLYN

Let me help you out. I'll be right back.

BROOKLYN located and returned from the office with the lone promotional copy of the Candy Girl Album in the city. It had been shipped to her from a DJ in Brooklyn.

BROOKLYN

No one in the whole city has this. Nobody. But you're special. Take your time. Look it over.

LITTLE BOY took it and looked at the front and then the back of the LP, taking his time to look at the pictures and read the name of each song.

LITTLE BOY
Can I listen to it?

BROOKLYN
"Who's Loving You." Hmmm, that's a pretty heavy song young man. Something on your mind?

LITTLE BOY
I don't know. It reminds me of someone I hadn't thought about in a while.

BROOKLYN
A special friend?

LITTLE BOY
Yeah. Real special. I lost her a few months ago. She was the one that really got away.

BROOKLYN
Girlfriend?

LITTLE BOY
Huh?

BROOKLYN
Was she your girlfriend?

LITTLE BOY
Oh no, never, she's an angel.

BROOKLYN

Oh, she's very special.

LITTLE BOY

Yeah. But even if hadn't been an angel, she couldn't have been my girlfriend. My Mother told me I couldn't have a girlfriend until I had a place of my own, a job, a car, and most importantly a savings account.

(BROOKLYN smiled. She recognized that LITTLE BOY was serious about his status and the status of the girl.)

BROOKLYN

You got any of those yet?

LITTLE BOY

Nope. Not one.

BROOKLYN

But you're working on them, right?

LITTLE BOY

Me? I'm twelve. But one day I'll have them all. I'm going to get out of here and when I do, I'm going to grab this world by the tail just like my friend Otis used to. And I'm going to shake it just like this. (LITTLE BOY demonstrated the maneuver to BROOKLYN.)

BROOKLYN

My Dad said the desire to be great is what separates boys from men.

LITTLE BOY

Really, well I got a lot of desire in me. I'm going to be a man's man one day.

BROOKLYN

I can see it you Romeo. I just know you are. You got a real serious side to you too. Almost too serious at times. You need to smile more. Let me see that smile of yours.

(LITTLE BOY flashed his signature 10-watt half-smile.)

BROOKLYN

You must be saving your smiles for someone special. Your face is trying but your heart just ain't in it. I want to use some of that desire to show me the smile you put on that pretty brown face for the real special people in your world.

BROOKLYN squeezed his cheeks and gave him a sample of the good ole Queen City charm she had recently acquired. LITTLE BOY didn't realize it, but the unfamiliar look on display on his "pretty" brown face was him blushing. SISTER GIRL would later call it cheesing.

BROOKLYN

Stay right here. Don't move a muscle. I'm going to get my polaroid. I want you to have proof for the people that you haven't met yet, that you have an amazing smile. Even though you don't have perfect teeth.

(LITTLE BOY looked slightly puzzled.)

BROOKLYN returned with her Polaroid and snapped two pictures of LITTLE BOY. She gave him one and kept the other for herself.

BROOKLYN

Promise me you won't lose this.

LITTLE BOY

I promise.

BROOKLYN

Good. Let's go play your song. (BROOKLYN guided LITTLE BOY towards the turntable.) What's your name by the way?

LITTLE BOY

Little Boy.
(BOOKLYN stared at LITTLE BOY waiting for the punchline that never came.)

BROOKLYN

What's your real name?

LITTLE BOY

Little Boy is my real name.

BROOKLYN

OK that's unexpected. A little different but it totally fits you.

(BROOKLYN chuckled and poked LITTLE BOY in the ribs with her elbow just to show him she understood.)

BROOKLYN

Listen up Record Theater, this next song is going out to my new best friend in the whole wide world. The young man they call Little Boy.

Everyone in the store clapped. It was a tradition. For just a moment, LITTLE BOY felt the acceptance and approval he desperately sought inside 8 Trammell Walk.

"Who's Loving You" flowed out the overhead speakers and straight into LITTLE BOY's soul.

BROOKLYN had her eyes focused on LITTLE BOY's face and immediately noticed the effect the words had on him.

His half smile had been replaced by an upside-down crown and a river of tears began to flow over and down his cheeks. Leaving a stream between his feet.

(BROOKLYN rushed to him and held him closely.)

BROOKLYN

Heyyyy, Little Boy. I got you. It's going to be OK. You're safe. Just wait right here. I'm going to turn it off right now. Don't go anywhere. I'll be right back. OK?

LITTLE BOY

OK. I'll be....(Between tear drops and sobs.)

BROOKLYN

You don't have to talk. Just don't leave.

BROOKLYN stopped the song mid play and switched to something light and airy. Jazz. Then she returned to LITTLE BOY with a box of tissues.

BROOKLYN

You lost her, lost her. I thought you meant you two weren't friends anymore. You're still hurting Little Boy. It's called grieving. Has anyone ever talked to you about grieving?

LITTLE BOY

No.

BROOKLYN

That's why you rock that half smile. I bet you haven't cried yet. Have you?

LITTLE BOY

No.

BROOKLYN

You've got to cry Romeo. You've got to get that hurt out of you. It hides behind those big ole brown eyes of yours and it can only get out through your tears. But you're still trying to hold onto them. Why?

LITTLE BOY

When I try to smile, I feel like I'm just trying to forget about her and that makes me think that she's looking at me and thinking that I don't care that she's gone. But Brooklyn I do care so I hold onto my smiles and my tears. It's so confusing. I'm so lost in it all.

BROOKLYN

It doesn't work like that Little Boy. When you cry you allow your heart and your mind to speak to one another. When you let that happen, your heart can tell your mind that it's OK to be you again. You'll begin to realize that you can laugh and cry and all the things in between. They both know that those tears will carry most of that sadness right along with them. Then you can smile that beautiful smile of yours. If you believe. Do you believe?

LITTLE BOY

Can you say that again?

BROOKLYN

All of it?

LITTLE BOY

The part where my heart talks to my mind.

BROOKLYN

Of course. The short version. Crying is the way the mind and the heart talk. It's the way the heart lets the mind know it's OK to laugh and cry again. Do you understand?

LITTLE BOY

I think I so. No one ever talks to me about all the feelings I have floating inside my head.

BROOKLYN

That's not true anymore. I'm talking to you. Just realize that every question we ever have in this life will be answered in its own time.

We just have to have patience. Some call it faith which is nothing more than your trust that the one that made you will complete you. Look at those eyes. They're beautiful. One day, the one He made just for you, is going to get lost in them.

LITTLE BOY

Oh, you got jokes about my big eyes too. Are you trying to say they're sooooo big that a girl will literally get lost in them?

BROOKLYN

That's not what I meant. You are definitely all boy. Literal all the time. But now that you mention it. Come a little closer so I can see if there's a girl already trapped in them.

She reached for his face and in the twinkle of an eye everything in his reality had changed. She held his face in her hands. No one had ever gotten that close to him.

BROOKLYN

Are you OK? You froze there for a moment. Did I do something wrong?

LITTLE BOY

(LITTLE BOY blurted it out.) Everyone that gets close to me either lies to me or leaves me. (Pulling himself away from her.)

BROOKLYN

WOW. I didn't know. You've been hurt really bad, haven't you?

LITTLE BOY

Yes, but I don't want to talk about it.

BROOKLYN

It's OK. You don't have to talk about it. Let's just leave it right here for now. What you need right now is a strong drink podner. Let's pony up to the bar and get you a tall root beer in a real dirty glass. (LITTLE BOY laughed a little laugh.)

BROOKLYN returned with LITTLE BOY's root beer in a tall brown glass (dirty). She had broken the ice blockage inside his mind just like that. This was her gift. Her superpower. The ability to uplift. LITTLE BOY gulped it down and let out a big belch. Without thinking about it. His mood had shifted.

BROOKLYN

Do you feel better now?

LITTLE BOY

Yes. Thank you. How did you do that?

BROOKLYN

I didn't do anything you wouldn't have done for me. You needed everything that did happen to happen. To become the man, you are destined to be, and I am glad I am part of our journey. That's what we do when we meet another on our path. We share the load.

LITTLE BOY

Wow, He sent you all the way from Brooklyn to the Queen City to tell me this.

BROOKLYN

Remember this Little Boy. To most of the people in the world you may just be something they can take or leave but to a small group of special people you're going to be everything they needed. Someone they couldn't have made it through the storm without. That group will never leave you.

(LITTLE BOY knew exactly what BROOKLYN meant as soon as she said it. He felt the warmth of MIKA's smile on his face.)

BROOKLYN

When do you plan on getting that job, a place, and that savings account?

LITTLE BOY

When I grow up, I guess.

BROOKLYN

Good answer. Don't rush. Whoever He makes for you will be there when you get there. I have a good feeling about that.

LITTLE BOY

This is so unbelievable.

BROOKLYN

What?

LITTLE BOY

You. Your words. She said I would know her by her words.

BROOKLYN

Your friend the angel?

LITTLE BOY

Yes. That's all I can say about it now.

BROOKLYN

That's cool. A young man with a little mystery behind him.

LITTLE BOY

Do you want to be my best friend?

BROOKLYN

Whoa hold your horses Cowboy. You can't come at a lady like that. You'll scare her off. A Lady wants to be pursued. She wants to know that you took the time to really discover if she could be your best friend. I got a lot to teach you Romeo. But to answer your question, I would love to be your friend.

LITTLE BOY

So, you're saying there's a chance you will become my best friend? (BROOKLYN giggled and pinched LITTLE BOY's cheeks for the last time of this day.)

BROOKLYN

All I can say right now is that you are going to do some great things on this Earth, and it will be my pleasure to say that I've known you for as long as I've known you. Thanks for making a lady smile. I'm going to write you a short letter. Make it a note. Something else you can hold onto to remember this day.

BROOKLYN wrote the note on a napkin at the counter. It said LITTLE BOY will you be my friend, yes or no. There was a large box next to the words yes and no.

LITTLE BOY took it and read the first "love" note he would receive in this life. He put a big ole X in the box marked yes and handed it back to BROOKLYN. She kissed the note with her amazing lipstick and handed it back to LITTLE BOY.

BROOKLYN

Keep this. Look at it whenever you need to know that someone in this world thinks that you are AMAZING. If you lose it or the picture I gave you, we're going to have a major problem when we meet Little Boy.

LITTLE BOY

Major?

BROOKLYN

Major...

(BLACKOUT)

(END OF SCENE)

(END OF ACT)

ACT 3

Scene 1
PAUL

SETTING: Another summer had finally come to an end. It had been a most difficult year for LITTLE BOY. MIKA had gone on to live among the stars and every day after that one was difficult. LITTLE BOY was so alone and forever cloaked in darkness. School was around the corner and a certain Miss Indian Summer had arrived to wrap the Queen City in one of her thicker blankets.

LITTLE BOY hated this time of year more than all the rest. Not because it was hot. It marked the beginning of a new season of depression. The annual return to the criminal indoctrination process masquerading as an educational system didn't help matters. LITTLE BOY felt like a political prisoner locked in a cell that no one else could see.

The warden's schedule never changed. Wake up. Press play. Leave home. Sit down. Shut up. Raise your hand. Bell sounds. Stand up. Shuffle along. Sit down. Shut up. Rinse and repeat six more times each day. Last call. Press stop. Get up. Take home more work. Got to sleep. It's just Monday.

LITTLE BOY would do this, eight hours each day, five days a week, for forty weeks. He still had 6 years remaining on this 12-year bid and there was no possibility for early release for good behavior. He had known shooters, the young guns, who had done less time for doing much worse.

They told LITTLE BOY that he was young, black, and gifted. That was the label that they gave him. The reward for achieving this status. But what were the other little brown faces he spent his time with outside the lab called? Young, black, and ordinary? The label had changed everything. His life was no longer his own. He had won some "invisible lottery" and received entry into a lifetime of assimilating, introduced to the peculiars of a most unwanted American experiment.

One where "allegedly brilliant" educational social engineers sat in sterile pseudo think tanks and thought that removing the best and brightest little brown boys and girls from their neighborhood schools and shipping them off to neighborhoods that did not desire them on yellow "school" buses would somehow improve the lot of the little brown faces who became citizens of the village.

The crisp white walls made his small copper-colored face stick out like a dwarf star in a sky full of curious white luminaries.

From day one LITTLE BOY knew that fitting in was going to be a problem. He had no space of his own. His skin, his hair, his lips, his "accent" invited unwanted attention.

There was nothing that could hide LITTLE BOY's most glaring markers. That he was poor and bitter, and those two forces left marks that colored his thoughts, actions, and words.

While the brown faces that looked the part. Wrapped in polo, Levi's, and Nikes, basked in the glory of their new celebrity status. LITTLE BOY sat alone, dreaming, and praying that no one, brown or white, noticed him. He knew they knew he wasn't from Mayberry. Not by a long shot.

He remembered Otis on the tough days and hid his rose deep inside himself. If he had to do the time, he would do so on his own terms, locked away in solitary. They could view his shell but the part that was really his belonged only to him.

And just when he had mastered his daily routine there came a new cocoa brown face who had the ability to see where LITTLE BOY had hidden himself. This was unexpected. Mika was the only person who had this ability. LITTLE BOY was silently intrigued. This kid had his own style. His hair was so different. LITTLE BOY wondered if this was how the light bright kids felt when they looked at his hair. He also wondered if they had been labeled young, white, and gifted.

LITTLE BOY had never seen anything like this hair. Part afro, part unknown. It was poofy and shiny. The combination both puzzled and amazed LITTLE BOY. The kids name was Paul.

LITTLE BOY would later rename him Paulie because that's what he did. He renamed everyone who was important to him. Anyone who left their mark on his rose.

LITTLE BOY liked PAUL from the moment they met, he was different and when he was around LITTLE BOY felt less alone. The outcast was no longer the only one who refused to drink from the cup of his story.

At RISE: LITTLE BOY is seated on the edge of one of the two inexpensive twin beds in the small bedroom he shared with LITTLE BROTHER. The walls were various shades of white. There was no glam nor glory in the Gardens.

LITTLE BOY lived in a row house apartment deep in the projects on the Queen City's east side. The other side of the tracks.

PAUL is seated downstairs at the kitchen table, in a cozy 4-bedroom home way out in the suburbs. On the north side. Across tracks LITTLE BOY had never discovered. Or so LITTLE BOY had been led to believe.

LITTLE BOY imagined that PAUL walked around in a smoking jacket with a small bell in hand. A bell he used frequently to signal the butler who addressed his every need.

Try as he might LITTLE BOY could never imagine the butler being anything but black. Any other reality was simply out of the question.

PAUL was the only child of two teachers. A cruel twist of fate for any child forced into the digesting the propaganda that was public school indoctrination.

Where could he escape from their clutches? Education had its own seat at the table and was extra attentive whenever grades were discussed and the expectations of the two teachers were made crystal clear.

PAUL managed it well most of the time. He was often stable. Test days, now they were a little different, and if you probed you got the sense that he wasn't always sure he was capable.

LITTLE BOY had become a means of destressing for PAUL in those moments. They were boys who often carried the weight of men on their tiny shoulders. Born to two different mothers, they were much more than just friends. They were Hip and Hop. Fists in the air, pinky swear, for life.

Between the two houses laid a single track, a metaphor of sorts, with a sign above it, that read "Tomorrow 6 Miles." A message to anyone paying attention that you are neither your beginning nor your present. Tomorrow brought with it new possibilities.

LITTLE BOY dialed the numbers to PAUL's home. PAUL had scribbled it on a torn piece of paper during homeroom. This was a new experience for LITTLE BOY. The phone wasn't a constant in LITTLE BOY's home. It appeared and disappeared like a blue moon. Unfortunately, when LITTLE BOY needed the blue moon the most it couldn't be found.

After he spun the last digit, a nine, the phone rang on the other end, and the Polite home sprang into action. This was part of the evening's entertainment. The phone sang loudly initiating a series of events that would make both boys laugh like each time was the first time.

(The phone rang loudly on the wall about two feet away from where Paul sat.)

MRS. POLITE

(From the living room.) Paul, the phone is ringing.

(The phone continues to ring.)

MRS. POLITE

Paul, can you get that?

(Crickets.)

The phone finally stopped ringing on the seventh ring. Mrs. Polite had to answer it again.

MRS. POLITE

Paulllllll.

There was weight in MRS. POLITE's pretty voice, but the presence of agitation could never be found within her words. Mrs. Polite could have been a distinguished member of the Customer Service Hall of Fame. LITTLE BOY imagined how his mother would have managed this situation. (LITTLE BOY laughs quietly.)

PAUL

Yeah Mom. (As he looked at the phone.) Who is it?

MRS. POLITE

There's someone named Little Roy on the phone.

PAUL

Who?

MRS. POLITE

Hold on. Young man could you please tell me your name again?

LITTLE BOY

Yes Ma'am. My name is Little Boy.

MRS. POLITE

(To Paul.) He said his name is Little Boy not Little Roy.

PAUL

Ohhh Little Boy. That's my man. I got it. (Paul picked up the receiver from the wall.)

MRS. POLITE

OK, I'm hanging up the phone now. (Speaking to herself.) Now that's a different name. Little Boy That's my man... These kids think they're so cool. They are so funny.

PAUL waited 20 seconds before he said another word. This was a habit. MRS. POLITE's delayed signoffs would become some of their most epic comic relief moments.

PAUL

Yo, I didn't know you actually went by Little Boy to everyone.

LITTLE BOY

Why wouldn't I? It's my name.

PAUL

Why wouldn't you? Let me see. How about that's not a real name.

LITTLE BOY

It's real to me. More real than Paul. Think about it, would you really have picked Paul if you had a choice?

PAUL

I don't know.

LITTLE BOY

You mean you really like Paul?

PAUL

Man get off my name. That's my father's fathers name.

LITTLE BOY

Meaning it's not yours, is it?

PAUL

I guess not Mr. Boy.

LITTLE BOY

It's Mr. Blue. It's alright you'll be free one day.

PAUL

Oh snap. Freedom. From whom my parents? Damn, I'm a slave to them too?

LITTLE BOY

Aren't all kids Paul?

PAUL

Sure.

LITTLE BOY

You know I can see things in people that they can't see in themselves.

PAUL

Oh yeah, so what can you see through the phone?

LITTLE BOY

I know that sometimes you feel like baby Jesus trying to hide among them Egyptians.

(PAUL didn't know at the time that LITTLE BOY talked plurality.)

PAUL

Man, you are crazy. What the hell are you talking about now? (The two liked trying out their cool cuss words.)

LITTLE BOY

My message is clear.

PAUL

It's not. So, break it down a for a brotha. Maybe my thoughts are not your thoughts. Or as you said, it's one of those things I just can't see in myself.

LITTLE BOY

Let's say, once upon time, little baby Paul was whisked away from the hood only to find himself in a cold, cold, world where no one looked like him, spoke like him, or thought like him. And maybe, just maybe, being the only one of your kind all the time, became a bit much for the little baby Paul to handle.

PAUL

Damn. OK you read my palm. Why don't you tell me the rest of my story?

LITTLE BOY

Even if I could, I wouldn't do that. You gotta live this life. No one can see their future. Our stories write themselves by our decisions and actions.

PAUL

Well, ain't that inconvenient. Your "skills" only work when you look behind you.

(The two boys cracked up.)

LITTLE BOY

You have the same skills. Tell me what you see in me.

PAUL

Man, your book is sealed. You say just enough to disguise the reality that you don't really say anything at all.

LITTLE BOY

Keep going.

PAUL

You mean I'm right?

LITTLE BOY

You might be. Who can know these things? It is interesting to hear though. Please continue. This must be what therapy feels like.

PAUL

With you. Nothing seems to matter. It's like you can take it or leave it most of the time. Things could be this or that. Hot or cold. But the only side you're on is your own.

LITTLE BOY

Ouch... How did that feel?

PAUL

What?

LITTLE BOY

Saying what you really feel.
PAUL

It's different. A little uncomfortable. I just realized that I never really do that. We just tell little white lies, to one other, all the time. That's so crazy. But I like this real talk. You're a different kind of brother.

LITTLE BOY

A weirdo, right?

PAUL

Nah just different. It's like you're looking at life through 3-D glasses. (LITTLE BOY nodded his head slowly as he pondered PAUL's words playing air drums as he looked out the window.)

PAUL

Man, I hate having to be the one to tell you this. But you're going to be misunderstood a lot. I know twelve-year-olds aren't ready for you. I don't think teachers are ready for your thoughts either.

LITTLE BOY

Really?

PAUL

Yeah. How are you going to handle that?

LITTLE BOY

I don't know. Stay to myself.

PAUL

How can you stay any more to yourself than you do now? What happens when it ain't safe for you to be there by yourself?

LITTLE BOY

Paul, what are you talking about?

PAUL

Man, you got siblings. I don't. I spend most of my time at home talking to myself. It ain't a good feeling. I hate it. I can't imagine if I had to spend even more time alone with myself. That ain't good and I like who I am.

LITTLE BOY

Oh, and I don't? Hopefully, Mr. Polite, someone will be there who really knows me. Someone who can sense that I am in a little trouble. Someone like you maybe.

PAUL

You know I got your back Little Boy. I promise you if I see something, I'm going to say something and if you call me, I'll be there. I won't leave you hanging.

LITTLE BOY

Hmmm. You mean you're going to answer the phone before the seventh ring?

PAUL

Either me or my mother.

LITTLE BOY

Oh yeah, I forgot you had a secretary. You know that ain't right man.

PAUL

You mean you don't have one?

LITTLE BOY

No. That don't go on this side of the tracks. I needed to hear your words. Most of the time being alone is my safe place, Sometimes, she ain't safe though and it's hard to know when she is and when she isn't.

PAUL

Like I said, your thoughts aren't my thoughts. You over there. I'm over here. Are you safe now? Are you sad?

LITTLE BOY

I don't know. Most of the times I'm something else. Something worse than sad. Sometimes I'm just nothing.

PAUL

Man, you're somebody. You're Little Boy. Everyone likes you.

LITTLE BOY

No one even knows me, Paul. How can they like someone they don't know? Man, I know me, and I don't even like me most of the time.

PAUL

I don't know what to say to that. You're twelve man. It can't be that serious. What could make you feel like this? When you talk like this am I supposed to keep these things to myself?

LITTLE BOY

You're my friend, aren't you? I can't answer your riddle. Right now, I just feel safe being able to tell someone how I'm feeling. Maybe all you're supposed to do is listen to me. Maybe you're here to tell everyone that I was here.

PAUL

Yo man. What's that supposed to mean? That's not a riddle. What happens if something happens to you? Am I supposed to hold on this feeling for the rest of my life?

LITTLE BOY

What are you feeling?

PAUL

Uneasy.

LITTLE BOY

Man, I'm nobody. The saddest thing in the world is to be here and feel like no one cares that you exist. I don't know how I even got here. I don't know what I'm saying. I can't be the only one that feels this and I'm tired of feeling it.

(LITTLE BOY started sobbing.)

PAUL

Are you crying? Yo, what's really going on man? I thought we were just going to talk and laugh at people. Come on man. Say something. You know we got gym tomorrow and you know Mr. Stevens is going to set up the horses for vaulting. You know he knows brothers don't vault. But that's Mr. Stevens. He knows we'll be sitting in the bleachers laughing like we do taking an F for the team. OK, this is the part where you're supposed to laugh. This is the part where you always laugh. Yo, I need you to laugh Little Boy. Did you hear me? I said I need to hear you laugh.

(Eerie silence.)

PAUL

This is getting weird and you're starting to scare me. If you don't say something, I'm going to put my mom on the phone. Trust me, you don't want that. She'll have cops knocking on your door. You said you needed someone to listen. I'm listening. But if this is going to work, if you're going to feel like this sometimes, it has to be a two-way street. You have to care enough about me to listen to me too and you can't just shut down and go silent after you unload something like this on me. You need a safe place to get things off your chest, I can be that, but I need to feel safe too. I need to know you're not going to do something crazy because this is a lot to take in. Do I need to call my mom?

LITTLE BOY

No. I'm listening.

PAUL

Are you OK?

LITTLE BOY

Yeah. I'm OK. (In a shallow voice. It was the first time he had lied to PAUL. (It wouldn't be the last.) Man, I gotta go.

PAUL

Nah man we're not done.

LITTLE BOY

I'm done.

(CLICK!)

PAUL

(Still holding the receiver to his ear.) Well damn...

Paul knew they would never talk like this again. Two boys, brothers from different mothers, living on opposite sides of the tracks, sat, and rained tears for reasons neither could articulate.

Life...

(BLACKOUT)

(END OF SCENE)

ACT 3

Scene 2
LYFE

SETTING: Even though LITTLE BOY had only lived twelve years; he had lived long enough to know that the enemy never fights fair. He never had to. Because no one truly believes that he exists. Try as hard as you might to broach the subject with others. The more you tried to talk about him the less people wanted to hear.

Despite these things, LITTLE BOY never, ever, stopped fighting him. He never came in person. He did his dirt though others.

LITTLE BOY knew that one day they would meet. He had always known this. His whole life hung on this belief. There was nowhere he went that he didn't sense his presence.

He would never have chosen the path of avoidance. Someone had to stand up to him. But death was the one thing that could detour him from his destiny. Death offered something that the enemy nor life had in their possession. Death could reunite him with Mika.

LYFE knew this and LYFE arrived in the place of the Enemy and Death. LITTLE BOY didn't know the difference. LITTLE BOY had neither met LYFE nor the Enemy. Therefore, in anticipation of meeting Death. He was happy to meet this mystery man.

He would never have chosen the path of avoidance. Someone had to stand up to him. But death was the one thing that could detour him from his destiny. Death offered something that the enemy nor life had in their possession. Death could reunite him with Mika.

LYFE knew this and LYFE arrived in the place of the Enemy and Death. LITTLE BOY didn't know the difference. LITTLE BOY had neither met LYFE nor the Enemy. Therefore, in anticipation of meeting Death. He was happy to meet this mystery man.

LYFE had been the bigger mystery to LITTLE BOY. A riddle that was more pain than pleasure? It seemed that the tighter you held on to it, the faster it slipped through your fingers. It was like grasping for air or holding water.
And even when you thought about waving goodbye to LYFE, designating it as a ride you would rather not take. The reality that you had to ride it in order to make that claim hit him right smack dab in the middle of his heart.

LITTLE BOY hated the feeling of not being in control. He had nowhere to place the weight of this hate. So, he walked alone with it. Carrying it day after day, month after month, and year after year.

Growing old before his time. But he would not pass this burden on to another. This battle would be fought by him and no other. Or so he thought.

At RISE: LITTLE BOY is seated on his favorite bench. playing WANDA like it would be the last time. It was a bright and sunny day. The song had no beginning nor end. It had always been there. Buried deep down inside him.

In a place he had once known. A place that only he knew about. If it was going to go down. It was going to go down here. With his song.

As LITTLE BOY played his song a stranger entered the park from his right. Dressed in all black. He was well dressed fella. A familiar unfamiliar. His feet moved to the rhythm of LITTLE BOY's beat. It was as if he knew the notes before he played them.

Even the improvisations. This surprised LITTLE BOY who looked at him through his shades. His feet matched LITTLE BOY's rhythm note for note. He heard his song, and he followed LITTLE BOY's lead.

You can learn a lot about someone if you sit quietly and watch them long enough. He knew LITTLE BOY was special. Not so much for what he could do or achieve. But more so for all the little boys that he could one day inspire to cross over their pain, to cross the bridge, and get to the other side.

LITTLE BOY had the ability to show others that there were far greater options than jumping from the bridge. He could help them figure out the riddle that played non-stop inside their mind. Consuming their time. Driving them crazy.

As LITLE BOY played, LYFE seemed to float over to the bench stopping behind him, right next to the two sentries. He reached out and touched the streetlight and just like that the sun gave up its light. Transferring its dominion to the lesser light which now blazed the evening sky. A sentry standing guard behind the bench. Like LYFE it had changed in the blink of an eye.

LITTLE BOY
Whoa, where did the sun go?

LYFE
Don't worry, it will be back tomorrow.

LITTLE BOY
Are you the one I've been waiting for?

LYFE
Yes.

LITTLE BOY
You're not what I imagined?

LYFE
What did you imagine?

LITTLE BOY
That you would look different.

LYFE
How so?

LITTLE BOY
Colder. Like the end of days.

LYFE
You were expecting someone else.

LITTLE BOY

Yes, and you're not him.

LYFE

No. Far from it.

LITTLE BOY

Then who are you?

LYFE

You don't know?

LITTLE BOY

No sir. I do not. I've never seen you before.

LYFE

Interesting.

LITTLE BOY

Why?

LYFE

You could say there is no me without you.

LITTLE BOY

Then why don't I know you?

LYFE

Oh, but you do. Let me hold Wanda.

(LITTLE BOY handed WANDA to LYFE. LYFE began to play notes from a song that LITTLE BOY had buried inside himself. Notes that LITTLE BOY had never played before another.)

LITTLE BOY

How do you know my song?

LYFE

How do I?

LITTLE BOY

I don't know. I've never played it for anyone.

LYFE

Perhaps.

(LITTLE BOY felt aggravation creeping in. He hated it when questions were answered with questions.)

LITTLE BOY

Why are you here? What happened to the one I was waiting for?

LYFE

Hold your horses. I came here for answers too.

LITTLE BOY

I didn't come here to talk to you.

LYFE

Are you sure about that? What is death but the absence of life? You can't meet him until you've let go of me.

LITTLE BOY

Great another riddle.

LYFE

No. This isn't a game. I'm here because if you want to end this conversation you have to tell me to go.

LITTLE BOY

You're grown and I'm twelve. You don't need my permission to leave.

LYFE

Who owns the future? The man or the little boy inside him?

LITTLE BOY

What do you mean?

LYFE

Does the little boy live inside the man, or does the man live inside the little boy?

LITTLE BOY

Why are you trying to confuse me?

LYFE

I'm not. You know what I'm saying. I want you to listen to what I say next. You have a lot of shades Little Boy. From some angles all I see is Mika. Her spirit is all over you. Sometimes when I close my eyes all I can hear is Otis. Talking about a rose that life couldn't destroy. Then there are times I feel Lisa's presence within you. A warm embrace that the broken so desperately need. She calms you down just enough to get you through those tough times. When I allow myself to dream, my dreams are of Little Brother and Big Sister and a future that takes you outside these bricks. Neither you nor the man you become want a future without them there. What I'm saying Little Boy, is there are so parts of you that aren't you. The special ones leave a part of themselves inside you. Things that are meant to be shared with the world. The answer to your riddle is this. The man is nothing without the little boy.

LITTLE BOY
Ohhhhhhhh.

LYFE
Sometimes we dwell on the bad things, because they hurt so much that they make us forget about all the beautiful people and things we have in our lives. The ones who took the time to leave something beautiful within us. A part of themselves, that they deposit inside us, their very own safety deposit box. Sometimes it's their last deposit, sometimes it's their only precious jewel. And they choose to leave it with us. The one thing they want shared with the world. Things they may not be able to share themselves. Choosing us to be the caretaker.

(She came down from the stars.)

MIKA
Hey Little Boy. You looking for me?

LITTLE BOY
Oh my GOD. Mika, is this really you? Did I die? Why are you here?

MIKA

Boy stop acting crazy. Yes, it's me and no you're not dead. Would this old and busted bench be among the stars? Why do you think I'm here? Haven't I always been there when you needed me the most? Are you alright? Why are you trying so hard to get to me?

LITTLE BOY

Too many questions Mika. Slow down.

MIKA

Feels a lot different when you're on the other end of it? Doesn't it?

LITTLE BOY

(LITTLE BOY and LYFE laughed the same laugh at the same time.) Well, it's good to see you still got your sense of humor. It's good to see you. I have missed you so much. I've been going through the motions without you. School sucks, kids are mean, and I still don't fit in anywhere. I want to be where you are.

MIKA

Come on Little Boy. Do you really think you're the only one who feels like you do? There are a million Little boys and little girls out there going through the same thing that you and I went through. Didn't we find each other?

LITTLE BOY

Yes. You felt like this too?

MIKA

Yes, I did. Until I found you. And after we found each other, did you ever feel the sadness you felt before we met? I'll answer for you because you're going to overthink it like you do. No, you didn't, and neither did I. We didn't remember the sadness because we found life Little Boy.

(LITTLE BOY and LYFE nodded in agreement.)

MIKA

I wasn't the last of your discoveries. I was the first of many.

LITTLE BOY

Are you just saying that to make me feel good?

MIKA

NO. You know I don't care about your little ole feelings. (As she reached for his cheeks.) I came to remind you of something you once knew but forgot. It wasn't meant for me to walk the whole way with you and from what I know now about life, no one will ever walk every step with you, and you won't walk the whole way with another either. We're all like trains and people get on and get off at their stops. But the impact we have on one another lasts forever. Because during those short rides we share the best and the worst of ourselves. The good and the bad. The crookeds and the straights. You gave me something amazing and I have taken that part of you with me to the stars and it makes me and everyone around me smile Little Boy. My hope is that you never stop giving, that you stop chasing me, and that you share the part of me that I wrote on your heart with others like us. We're not misfits. We're treasures and kids like us are worth looking for. I'm sorry I didn't say all this to you in the hospital. I wouldn't have finished, and I didn't want your last memory of me to be one that would hurt you for the rest of your life. Please promise me that you will keep looking for them. The lost boys and girls of the world. You weren't made to chase me. You are a gift to be shared with the world.

LITTLE BOY

Thank you, Mika. Will I see…

MIKA placed a finger on LITTLE BOY's lips and whispered something in his ear. In a flash of light, she was gone, and LYFE began to play another song. A song LITTLE BOY recognized. It was OTIS's Rose.

OTIS entered the park dressed in all white. He was immaculate. Complete with top hat, tails, and a crystal cane. His steps were flawless, and, in his hand, he carried the most beautiful white rose LITTLE BOY had ever seen.

OTIS

That's my song Little Boy. I heard it and I had to see who was playing it. Man, I love that song. It has brought me so much joy. Lifted me up when I was down and taken me even higher when I was up. I brought you this rose to say thank you. So much has changed for me because I met you. I came here to remind you of that.

(OTIS passed the rose to LITTLE BOY.)

LITTLE BOY

Thank you, Otis. It's beautiful. I don't know what to say.

OTIS

You don't have to say anything Little Boy. Your words are right here. (Placing his hand on his heart.)

And the tiny warrior and the old soldier didn't say another word. OTIS was overjoyed, looking at the glow the rose put on LITTLE BOY's face.

At the time he picked it he didn't understand why, but this picture told him everything he needed to know.

It spoke words that would last an eternity. As LITTLE BOY sat and marveled at the rose, with a smile bright enough to light up the night, OTIS stood and hugged LYFE. He proceeded to dance the dance to his song, knowing he had gone where his feet were directed, and delivered the message he had been given.

(She walked back out of the Bayou.)

OTIS

Hey Little Lady.

LISA

Hello Mister Otis.

Otis and Lisa stepped to a beat right out of the French Quarter. LITTLE BOY couldn't believe his eyes. Lisa's moves were better than Soul Train. When they finished their steps, OTIS escorted LISA over to LITTLE BOY. He bowed and tipped his hat. LITTLE BOY stood and hugged LISA and they touched foreheads. Just like the last time. It was their thing.

LISA

Little Boy, a little yellow bird told me you were looking for me. He knocked right on my windowsill. I went right to my closet. Because I wanted to look special for you. As soon as I got the message, I knew a Lady looking this good would need an escort out of here, so I called Voice Magic and Hydraulic. You know they wouldn't miss this for the world. Lisa whistled.

The two superheroes walked in from the shadows. They glowed. Hydraulic was decked out in chrome from head to toe. Voice Magic was immaculate in his B-Boy stance, still possessing the most amazing pipes. It was the first time LITTLE BOY had ever seen them together. They were a dynamic duo. A father and son, together, forever.

LITTLE BOY

HYDRAULIC AND VOICE MAGIC!!!!! OH MY GOSH!!!! (Like a kid who snuck inside a comic book.) I can't believe this.

LITTLE BOY jumped up from the bench, running in place, spinning round and round, happier than a kid on the last day of school.

HYDRAULIC

Young man I had to meet you. There wasn't anything that was going to keep me from getting out of that hospital bed today. Your words have been with me through every step of my rehab. I became Hydraulic and I wanted to thank you for lighting that fire, because our stories are not our own.

LITTLE BOY

I knew you could do it Hydraulic. I just knew it. The whole world was waiting on you.

HYDRAULIC

You were right. My whole world was waiting for me.

LITTLE BOY

Voicemagic, what can I say? Your kicks are spotless, those creases sharp enough to slice bread, and the afro is just perfect!

VOICEMAGIC

Little Man I'm so happy to have my dad back. Guess what? I have two turn tables and a microphone now. I've been throwing the most amazing parties in the middle of the blocks. They call me Voicemagic too. You knew they would. You got to check me out one day Little Man. I got a new mix for you. An original. It's hot. I call it A Little Boy's Blues. There's nothing like it because there's nothing like you.

LISA

Little Boy we all miss you. This world can't keep you down. We can't imagine a world without you in it.

(Little Brother approached the bench with a giant bag of red candy fish.)

LITTLE BOY

Hey Little Brother. You and those fish.

LITTLE BROTHER smiled and nodded. He sat right next to LITTLE BOY. It was Big Brother and Little Brother. Just the way it should be.

Straight out of Brooklyn came a fresh beat blaring out the boom box that VOICEMAGIC sat next to the bench.

SISTER GIRL

Heyyyyy. I like that. What's your name, boy? You're kinda cute. (SISTER GIRL snatched VOICEMAGIC's hand before he could answer, and they danced like they had danced this dance together forever.)

SISTER GIRL

Don't worry about the answer to my questions. I'll give you all the words you'll ever need.

LITTLE BOY simply shook his head, laughed at SISTER GIRL, and prayed for VOICEMAGIC. He had no idea where the journey would take him.

One by one they walked by and whispered something into LITTLE BOY's ear and exited the park. They were smiling. There were no stormy tears. Leaving him alone on the bench with LYFE. This was not the way LITTLE BOY thought this day would end. But it was the way it ended which meant it was the way it was supposed to be.

LYFE

Amazing people, right?

LITTLE BOY

Yes. How did I forget about them?

LYFE

It happens from time to time when we ball up inside our own darkness. Just remember that our lives are not our own when we love others, and they love us back. You thought you were alone. But you were never alone Little Boy.

LITTLE BOY

I know that now. Thank you for showing me. You know you never told me who you are? What's your name?

LYFE

I have been called many names. Just know that I exist, and I thought you should meet me if you were sure that you wanted to leave me. I came here with a heavy heart. I know I can't keep you here. I know you know that too. Your friends can't either. Are you staying or leaving? You can't hold them hostage. Have them go through every day carrying that burden.

LITTLE BOY

I know. I owe Paul a big apology. I left a mountain on his shoulders. I'm going to stay Paul. (Holding his little brown fist to the sky.) I'm going to fight my way through this. I heard everything I needed to hear today. Living ain't easy. But it's a whole lot easier when people love you and care about you.

LYFE

Yeah. It is going to hurt sometimes. But choose life anyway.

LITTLE BOY

I will.

LYFE

We're counting on it.

LITTLE BOY

We?

MIKA & OTHERS

Yes, we, Little Boy. (Voices from amongst the stars.)

(BLACKOUT)

(END OF SCENE)

(END OF ACT)

(END OF PLAY)